Maryse Lafr

International acclaim!

GREAT BRITAIN

'Interesting hero, deft plotting and good writing:
it all adds up to a sparkling debut.'
Times Literary Supplement

'An asterisk for future reference against the name
of Inspector Charlie Salter of the Toronto Met,
a solidly appealing newcomer.'
Observer

'The real interest lies in the social context created
for Inspector Charlie Salter. An interesting, round-
ed character emerges — we will hear more of him.
Another good debut.'
Yorkshire Post

'The well-cultivated university terrain also offers
the gifted Mr. Wright an opportunity to reveal his
freshness of invention.'
Financial Times

(please turn the page)

'The first novel by Toronto professor Eric Wright is a classic whodunit and marks the first time that a Canadian author has made the ranks of the prestigious Collins Crime Club, whose members have included Agatha Christie. Wright has created a delightful detective in Toronto police Insp. Charlie Salter.'

Maclean's

'What's even more special in Wright's accomplishment is the manner in which he's welded Salter's character with the story. The two — detective and plot — are inextricable . . . The book offers other pleasures. Wright's prose is clean, well-paced, often witty and occasionally elegant. And his sense of place is exact . . . But best of all is his invention of Charlie Salter.'

Toronto Star

'Plausible page-turner relying on craft rather than gimmicks . . . Wright plans further Salter novels. Judging by this one, they'll be worth the wait.'

Montreal Gazette

'A classic novel of detection . . . One waits anxiously for his next book and for a reappearance by Charlie Salter.'

Calgary Herald

...t the Gods Smiled

...rticularly puzzling murder case that Inspector Charlie Salter of the Metropolitan Toronto Police is assigned to solve: Professor David Summers of Douglas College, Toronto, has been found dead in his Montreal hotel room while attending a conference. The only tangible clues are a lipstick-marked glass and the whisky bottle that was used to crush Summer's skull — clues so banal that they present a challenge in themselves.

From four of the late Professor's academic colleagues who had also attended the conference, and with the aid of one of Montreal's detectives, 'Onree' O'Brien, Salter must try to piece together the pattern of the victim's last hours.

Salter discovers that one of Summers's colleagues hated him with a vengeance but for a reason that comes to light only late in the story. And any of the others, it seems, could have had less obvious motives for murder. As the investigation proceeds Salter becomes aware of the parallels between himself and the dead man. He finds he likes the Professor's friends and dislikes his enemies. He is intrigued by the girl who was his favourite student. In the end it is through these similarities in their lives that he discovers the killer.

Charlie Salter is a most engaging detective. Real promotion within the Force has eluded him thus far — a compliment, it might be said, to his personal originality. Mystery fans will be delighted to learn that there are more Charlie Salter stories to come, for in *The Night the Gods Smiled* Eric Wright combines a fine sense for life's small absurdities with a distinct flair for creating a story full of suspense.

ERIC WRIGHT

The Night the Gods Smiled

Introducing Inspector Charlie Salter

A Totem Book
TORONTO

First published 1983
by Collins Publishers
100 Lesmill Road, Don Mills, Ontario

This edition published 1984
by TOTEM BOOKS
a division of Collins Publishers

Canadian Cataloguing in Publication Data

Wright, Eric.
  The night the gods smiled

ISBN 0-00-222644-8

I. Title.

PS8595.R53N53 1984   C813'.54   C84-098376-X
PR9199.3.W74N53 1984

Printed in Canada

T. J. Press (Padstow) Ltd

For Valerie

CHAPTER 1

Charlie Salter usually woke up badly these days. The worst mornings were those after nightmares when it took him whole minutes to realize that he was awake in his own bed, that he had not killed anyone or committed any other desolating or irretrievable act. There were other bad ways of waking, including times like this one when he lay waiting for the memories of all his failures to fade into the daylight. His first failures at school ('as soon as anything gets hard, you want to drop it'), his aborted university career ('you never finish anything'), his first, foolish marriage which collapsed within a year, and finally, his failure at his job. Salter was a police inspector; he had been an inspector for five years and he would almost certainly remain one for another fifteen years until he retired, a long way short of his early estimate of himself. It was this last failure which burned at the centre of his waking world, illuminating the others as they emerged from the base of his skull.

His eyes opened and he set about making the world liveable again. Beside him, Annie slept on, and Salter shoved his hand under her nightdress (one of his favourites, a thick cotton one she had inherited from her great-aunt, more erotic in the act of being lifted than any negligée) and stroked her, casually at first and then methodically, until she opened her eyes. He continued to caress her, waiting for her to pull out of reach or offer herself to him. She did neither, simply lay there under his hand, awake now, but with her eyes closed. He stopped, and she said, 'You are going to be late.'

He gave her one last squeeze, then pushed her on her back and rolled on to her, kissing her hard, grinding

himself against her. This was all he needed. As his desire
awoke (no failure here, yet) the ghosts of his other failures
crept back underground for another day. Salter locked
himself around her in a last playful hug, just for good
measure, and sat up. The day could begin.

Downstairs, the door slammed. Seth, the younger of
their two sons, had returned from his paper route. Seth
was always back by seven o'clock. His fourteen-year-old
brother, Angus, worked a double route and would arrive
in another fifteen minutes. Salter swung his legs out of
bed and stood up. 'You want some juice?' he asked. His
wife turned away and pulled the covers up to her chin.
'Yes, please.'

In the kitchen, Seth was already eating the granary-
floor sweepings that were traditional in the family, a
mixture of grains and nuts that Annie compounded from
ingredients bought at the St Lawrence market, inedible
to Salter, but preferred by the boys to anything else.
Salter grunted at his son and poured some orange juice.
He filled the kettle from the hot-water tap to make some
coffee, and took the juice up to his wife.

She was half asleep again, and he stood watching her
come to life. As everyone reminded him repeatedly, she
was an astonishing forty-year-old, with the same
absolutely flawless, fresh complexion, the same short,
thick brown hair with no trace of grey, and most
astonishing of all, the same brilliantly white teeth as she
had when she was fourteen. She was not a beauty, but she
was as perpetually radiant as an advertisement for her
own cereal. As she sat up now and took her juice, the door
slammed downstairs once again as Angus returned.

'Big day?' she asked.

'No big days now,' he said as he moved into the
bathroom. 'As far as I know, all I have to do is show some
New York cops around the office.' He lathered his face
and tried to guess which of the seven disposable razors on

the edge of the bathtub was the sharpest.

'It's nice,' she said. 'You are always home on time.'

'So you've said.' Salter found a razor with an edge and began stroking off the stubble. Behind him, he heard her get out of bed and go downstairs. He finished shaving and put on his plain-clothes uniform: clean shorts and socks, yesterday's shirt, blue tweed jacket, grey pants, dark blue tie with red geese, and black shoes. After a tour of the second floor in which he switched off six lights and one running tap, he went downstairs, switching off two more lights on the way, and opened the front door to let in the cat which was howling on the doorstep. The two boys were eating their cereal watching a cartoon on television, and Salter switched that off, too. The day had proceeded normally so far, from despair to irritation; there was only boredom still to come.

'Duncan called,' Annie said, when he was seated with the paper and his coffee. 'He wants to confirm we'll be down for July 1st.'

'I wouldn't mind doing something else this year. We have a month. I wouldn't mind a change,' Salter said.

There was an uproar. Seth pleaded, in a whine, 'O -come - on - Dad - let's - go - to - the - Island, - please -Dad - please,' and so on. Angus said, 'Uncle Duncan said I could crew for him this year in the regatta.'

'Did he?' Salter responded to this last. 'Well, maybe you two could go, and your mother and I will take a trip.'

Annie looked concerned, and seeing this, Salter became further irritated. 'I'd like to see something other than the bloody Island while I still have a few teeth left,' he said, shaking out his paper. 'We've been to the Island for four years in a row, and most years before that, too.'

Annie said, 'Dad's had a bad winter. He isn't very well.'

'All right, all right. Could we talk about it tonight?' He glared at the boys who were waiting for him to concede.

The Island was Prince Edward Island, Annie's

birthplace and for generations the home of her family, the Montagus, a family that was prominent, ancient, and soaked in Island tradition. Two of her brothers were lawyers, her uncle was a judge, and her father a doctor who had given up medicine to devote himself to his real estate interests. He owned two gas stations, a street of houses in Charlottetown, a small lumber-mill, a fish-canning plant, and a resort hotel, one of the oldest in the Maritimes. It was in this hotel that Salter had met Annie one summer as he passed through on the run from the wreckage of his first marriage. Annie was helping to manage the hotel in an undefined but concerned capacity; she had registered him, taken his order for dinner, chatted to him on the hotel porch after dinner, walked with him along the beach at sunset, and, after three days, refused to join him in bed, but made it clear that there were other places, and other times. He felt himself blessed that the Island princess had fallen for him, and persuaded her, after the season was over, to move to Toronto to be near him.

In Annie's family there was a tradition that the girls spend a year away from the Island before they settled down, rather like a year of finishing school — in Toronto or Montreal, or even London. Before they left the Island for this last, safe fling, the girls usually got engaged to apprentice lawyers or doctors, often their childhood sweethearts, and they returned, on time, when the internship or the articling period was up, to set up house and cottage. Annie shook her family by not making any arrangements for her return, and appalled them by wanting to marry a Toronto police sergeant, but they were full of goodwill, and when Annie brought Salter home to the family church the following spring, they welcomed him and made him an honorary member of the clan.

Each year after that the Salter family made the trip to

the Island for the vacation. Sometimes they drove, though it took three days; more often they went by train and were met by Annie's brother with one of the cars that the family lent them for the holiday, along with the keys to the family guest cottage.

Salter had married a tradition, a tradition that Annie guarded with the resolution of a Colonial among the natives. They used some of the family silver on Sundays (old Great-grandmother Montagu having apparently had place-settings for about three hundred, a collection that was broken up when she died), and about their Toronto house were a number of pieces of dark, polished furniture that Annie had inherited from the family homes (there were no harvest tables or other pine pieces, for such peasant artifacts had not formed part of the Montagu world for the last century and a half). Annie ritualized their lives slightly, too. Once a week, on Saturday, she made the porridge she ate as a child, although no one liked it much. She cooked fish chowders a lot and baked her own bread, but since the Island has no cuisine except salt cod and potatoes, their meals, except for one or two dishes which she had borrowed from the other maritime provinces, were otherwise the same as if she had been born in Calgary.

Annie's family were well-bred, tactful, and keen to include Annie's choice in the clan. They absorbed Salter's family into their world of fishing, sailing, riding and perpetual lobster suppers as if he had paid dues. Most of the time Salter was happy to enjoy their world. Occasionally, impatient and constricted by it, he felt like the lone Christian in-law in a family of Jews, conscious of his uncircumcised state, his slightly albino look, and of the determination of his relatives never to let him feel like an outsider.

'We have to let Duncan know soon if we aren't coming,' Annie said, as Salter rose from the table. The guest cottage was free to them whenever they liked, but it was much in demand during the season.

Salter felt himself on the brink of going too far. Clearly his words had upset everybody slightly. That was enough.

'Tell him we'll come,' he said. 'But entertain the possibility that you and I might take off for a week, would you? We could have a mad fling in Moncton.'

'You'll be late,' she said. 'Don't work too hard.'

'Didn't I tell you?'

'Yes, I know Charles, but couldn't we talk about that soon, too?'

'About quitting? Go to work for brother Duncan? I'm a policeman.' He cut off any reply by walking out of the door.

Salter's household was in an Anglo-Saxon ghetto off Oriole Parkway in an area that not so long ago had been North Toronto. But with the expansion of the city after the war, accompanied more recently by the building of the subway to the perimeter, his neighbourhood found itself at the heart of the city. When they first moved to the area, Salter had driven to work like everybody else; now he left his car at home for Annie and took the subway. Once, for a month, he had tried cycling to work long before it became fashionable, but the city sloped the wrong way for him, so that while the ride to work was easy, the sweating uphill return came at the end of a long day.

This morning the train was crowded as usual, but he managed to get the connecting door at the end of the car to lean against, a desirable spot because it let him read the paper with both hands. As usual, there were far more young girls on the train than any other single group—the roads to downtown were still packed with automobiles occupied by lone males—and when the car filled up, Salter found himself agreeably wedged between a tiny,

pretty, Japanese girl who smiled at him to show she saw
no danger in him, and, on the other side, an equally
small Caucasian girl with a clean-smelling, frizzy head
that came to just below his nose. He put down his paper
to avoid mussing either of the heads beneath him and
concentrated on looking fatherly. As the train arrived at
his station he looked down to make sure he didn't crunch
any little feet as he shuffled forward. Both girls looked up
and smiled at him. The English are right, he thought.
They *are* birds.

He .arrived at the headquarters building, and was
greeted, as he was every morning, by Sergeant Frank
Gatenby, The Oldest Sergeant on the Force. Gatenby was
not really that; there were a number of sergeants older
than he, but he had earned the title by his white hair and
avuncular manner, which he had acquired before he was
forty. For a long time he had been The Oldest Constable
on the Force, then someone in a burst of sentimentality
recommended his promotion, and he had been given to
Salter as an assistant.

'Quite a lot on your plate this morning, sir,' he said.
'You'll be quite the busy boy today, all right.' He smiled
like a butler addressing the young master.

Salter took his mail: arrangements to be made for the
tidying up of Yonge Street for a visit by the Mayor of
Amsterdam (I'll put a tart in an armchair in all the shop
windows, he thought; that'll make his worship feel at
home); report requested on the value of police horses in
suburban plaza patrols; an inspection of gunshops to
make sure they weren't selling machine-guns to minors; a
committee to be formed to investigate complaints about
the police cafeteria; a request for information from the
Montreal police. A typical pile of rubbish.

For Salter had been put out to pasture. In one year he
had gone from being a power in the internal structure of

the Force to the status of a non-person, simply because he had backed the wrong man for Deputy Chief too enthusiastically and without regard for the consequences. Too young to retire, as his mentor had done, he was too old to shift careers. His future had been with the Force; now he had no future.

Salter looked at the last item. 'What's this, Frank? What information do they want in Montreal?'

'Who can say, sir?' Gatenby said. 'Who—can—say?' he repeated, pronouncing each word slowly as if at the conclusion of an intense metaphysical speculation that had occupied him all morning. 'They phoned before you came in. I'd only just arrived myself. A man was found dead in Montreal last weekend. One of ours. I mean a Toronto man, not one of our boys. There's a sergeant coming in on the Rapido after lunch, so Chiefie is putting him on to you.' 'Chiefie' in Gatenby baby talk was the Superintendent. The Deputy Chief of Police was called 'Deecee'. 'There's a lot going on today, sir, and I suppose they couldn't spare anyone else.' The sergeant smiled like a host of a children's TV show.

'When's he coming?'

'Two o'clock.'

'All right. Tell "Chiefie" I'll do it. You never know. It might be a real job.'

'Chiefie's up with the Commission, sir. I think he just thought you would.'

Salter always went out to lunch. He didn't enjoy the food or the horseplay in the canteen, which was probably, he thought, why he had been put on the committee to investigate complaints. On this day he walked through to Yonge Street to a store that sold out-of-town newspapers, bought the latest edition of the *Montreal Gazette* and took it into a coffee shop that specialized in corned beef sandwiches. He found what he wanted on page three, a

small item to the effect that one David Summers, of
Toronto, had been found with his skull fractured in a
Montreal hotel room. Police were investigating. Nice,
old-fashioned murder. Sex, money or what? Why did the
Montreal boys need help already? He paid for his food
and worked his way back across a number of parking lots
to his office.

Gatenby met him at the door. 'He's here,' he
whispered, pointing elaborately over his shoulder into the
office. Salter, resisting the temptation to put his finger in
his mouth and roll his eyes in wonder, contented himself
with walking past the sergeant into his office and holding
out his hand. Gatenby trotted behind. 'This is Inspector
Salter, Sergeant,' he said from under Salter's elbow. 'Cup
of tea, anyone? Coffee? No? I'll leave you alone, then, to
have your chat.'

When the door closed, both men sat down.

'Someone got clobbered, I hear,' Salter offered. 'How
can we help?'

'My name is O'Brien, Inspector. Henri O'Brien.'

'Sorry. Yes. Charlie Salter.'

O'Brien took some papers out of a large envelope he
was carrying. 'What we would like is some help with the
questioning.' He was a small, trim man, a few years
younger than Salter, with close-cropped hair and a
weatherbeaten look like a lumberjack or a sailor. He
handed Salter one set of papers and kept a similar set for
himself.

'Let's go over it first, Sergeant. I know nothing about
it. Start at the top.'

O'Brien started to read in slightly accented English.
'David Arthur Summers. Age 47. Married. One
daughter. Professor at Douglas College. Found dead in
the Plaza del Oro Hotel on Saturday, May 18, at 11 a.m.
by the maid. Cause of death—fractured skull, probably
caused by a whisky bottle found on the floor. Victim

naked except for a dressing-gown. Room contained the clothes he had been wearing in a pile on the floor, his suitcase, still unpacked, the whisky bottle, nearly empty, two glasses, one with lipstick. No sign of a struggle. Time of death, about twelve hours previously.'

Salter wasn't listening. He was watching O'Brien read from a typescript in French and translate it simultaneously into English. Was there anyone here who could do that, he wondered? His own copy was in English.

O'Brien stopped reading, and there was a long pause.

'All right,' Salter said. 'What do you know about him?'

'His wife came to Montreal for the identification,' O'Brien said. 'She told us Summers was in town for an academic conference. It began on Friday and was to last until Wednesday. She said Summers and his colleagues went to this conference every year at this time, when the term was over. It is held in a different place each year so they get to see the country. A little 'oliday before they go off for the big 'oliday in the summer.'

The two detectives, who each got five weeks' paid leave a year, smiled at each other.

O'Brien continued. 'I have a statement from her here. She was not a great deal of help. She didn't know any reason why anyone should kill her husband. We couldn't question her too hard, of course, because she was very upset. We'd like you to talk to her again, also.'

'All right. He picked up a whore who rolled him, right? The badger game. What's that in French?'

'The badger game, Inspector. But his wallet was still in his jacket, with over a hundred dollars in cash.'

'They got disturbed,' Salter offered.

'We know most of the hookers in the city, except the teenagers. We are checking. We don't know any killers among them.'

'Someone he knew, then. Some woman. An affair de cur.'

'What?'

'You know. An affair of the heart. Sounds silly in English. The lipstick looks pretty obvious.'

'The blows were heavy. The doctor said it was someone quite strong.'

'They all study martial arts these days, Sergeant. My wife can lift her end of a railway tie.'

'Yes? But do English professors get into fights with their lovers?'

'What difference does it make what he teaches?'

'I meant English-Canadian professors, Inspector. Though, as a matter of fact, he did teach English.'

'I see.' Salter paused. O'Brien had introduced East/West relations into the discussion. You Anglos are a mystery to us Québécois. 'I guess professors are the same everywhere, Sergeant. Give them three drinks and they smash each other's heads in.' Screw you, froggie, he thought.

'Yes. Sorry. But your sergeant said something about he had heard we had a "crime de passion" we needed help with. He said he thought that was allowed in Quebec. I thought he was making jokes. Maybe you and he together.'

'Frank is an asshole, O'Brien. That's why he makes the coffee. But he's harmless. We don't make fun of foreigners, even Canadian ones.'

'And you, Inspector? You are in the homicide department?'

'No. I'm not. I am what we call General Duties.'

'I see.' O'Brien looked around the room that Salter shared with Gatenby, at Salter's nearly bare desk, at the uncarpeted floor, at the room's single decoration—a photograph from a newspaper of Gatenby saluting with one hand while he held open the door of some royal duke's limousine with the other.

Salter thought: He thinks he's been fobbed off with me

and Frank. So he has. He said, loudly, 'You asked for help with the questioning. What else can we do? Check up on Summers? I'll put Frank on to it.'

'A bit more than that, Inspector. Some of our separatists are making noises. We have our hands full.'

'But they just lost a referendum!'

'Yes. It's made them angry. Like English soccer fans when their team loses. In England, I mean.'

Here we go again. 'Or like French hockey fans when Maurice Richard is suspended.'

'That's right, Inspector.' I remember that, too. Well, what with the separatists and one or two other things we have had no leave for a month, so we do not have much time for cases like this.'

'Besides, it's just unlucky that he was killed in Montreal, right?'

'Right. What I am concerned with is screwing up at the beginning. Look. Like this. This man, at a conference with his colleagues, is hit by an enemy, or a lover, or, maybe, a whore. But if it is someone he knew, then a stupid investigator might talk to the person right away and not know it. He might miss the signs. There it is. I am busy and I am French. You see what I mean?'

'Yes. You haven't got the experience to watch out for English liars. So you want me to do it.'

'Yes. If you can.' O'Brien grinned. 'All Anglos sound like liars to me,' he risked.

Salter laughed. 'That's exactly what my wife said the other day about the French MP's you see on TV. Especially the cabinet ministers.'

'Tell her she's right, will you? You can't trust any Frenchman in Ottawa.'

They sat there, grinning at each other.

Salter said, 'Let's get down to it, Onree. What you are asking me to do is take over the investigation from here and give it back when I've got something for you.'

'If you have the time and the men.'

'I've got me, and Frank, and all the time I need. Now, what else? The suitcase. Anything unusual in it?'

'Nothing. Underwear, shirts, socks, two books. What you could expect.'

'The wallet?'

O'Brien read from the list. 'One hundred and six dollars. Two credit cards. Two library cards. Driving licence. Some lottery tickets. Membership of a squash club. A dirty piece of paper with some numbers on it — they look like telephone numbers — some charge slips. Here.' He dug into the envelope again and produced the wallet. 'You'd better take it. Show it to the wife when you talk to her.'

Salter took the wallet and dropped it into a drawer. 'That's it then. Coffee now?'

'Tea, if you don't mind.'

'Frank!' Salter gave the order and waited until the door closed. 'Anything I can do for you here in town, Onree? You know Toronto?'

'Not much. I thought I would spend a few hours here. I have a reservation on the overnight train, so my evening is free. But you weren't expecting me, so just point me in the right direction and I'll leave you to solve my case.'

'Which direction is that?' Sherlock Holmes would have known. The tan, the windswept haircut — what did they point to? The harbour for a quick sail around the islands?

'Greenwood racetrack. I've never been to the races in Toronto.'

Of course. 'I've never been either. Would you like some company? I wonder what time they start.'

'Seven-thirty.'

'Ah. Well, then, we could go and have some dinner, and go out to the track afterwards.'

'Fine, Inspector.'

'Charlie.'

'Fine, Charlie. But why don't I come back at, say, five-thirty, and then we could go out and have dinner at the track.'

'I don't know if they have a restaurant, Onree.'

O'Brien looked knowing. 'They all have restaurants. I will be back at five-thirty.' He put his envelope back in his briefcase and shook hands with Salter.

When the door closed, Salter phoned his wife. 'I won't be home for dinner,' he said. 'I think I may have a real job.'

Annie said, 'Fraud, arson, robbery with violence?'

'Murder.'

'And they gave it to you!'

'It's not on our turf so "DeeCee" and "Chiefie" don't give a pinch. But it's just like a real job to me.'

'Now we start skipping dinner again? Working all night?'

'Not yet. But you never know. It might come to that. I hope so. Don't wait up. First, I'm going to the races. 'Bye, dear.' He hung up, agreeably mysterious.

Annie was waiting up for him when he got home.

'You look pleased with yourself,' she said. 'Did you win?'

'I didn't lose,' he said smugly, and waited to be asked again.

'How much?' she asked.

'A "C-note",' Salter said, out of the corner of his mouth like a regular gambler.

'Enjoy yourself?'

'Bloody marvellous. Want to hear about it?'

'Of course. I'll make some tea.'

What's going on with her? Salter wondered. She's acting strange.

'What's the matter?' he asked truculently. 'You jealous of my night out?'

'Don't be silly, Charlie. Just tell me about it. What happened?'

Salter gave a mental shrug and resumed his euphoric mood. 'The thing is,' he began. 'It's harness racing — you know — chariots.'

She nodded, a little girl hearing about Daddy's day.

'They have two kinds of horses — trotters and pacers — you know about this? The trotters move differently from the pacers.'

'They trot?'

'Yes.' What the hell was going on? 'They move diagonally, but the pacers move one side at a time — or is it the other way round? I couldn't really see the difference, even when I knew. Anyway, it's quite a sight when the lights go up and there they go.'

'Did you bet on every race?'

'Yes. Onree explained it to me . . .'

'Onree?'

'This Frenchman whose case I'm on. I picked out my own horses, though. I chose ones with names I liked, although the trouble was, half of them seemed to have similar names like Armbro or Hanover or something. Anyway, to make the story short, I won on seven races and picked up a hundred and twenty dollars. Onree lost fifty, betting on form. Ha, ha, ha. It was terrific. I would have won on eight but my horse stopped running properly — they had a name for what it did wrong.'

'Broke stride.'

'What?'

'It's called breaking stride.'

'How do you know?'

'They use the same term on the Island.'

Salter was dumbfounded. 'You mean those races in Charlottetown are the same as these?'

'That's right, Charlie. The races we've been trying to get you to come to for the last fifteen years. The trots, we call them. Daddy used to *own* a standardbred—that's what the horses are called. You have refused to have anything to do with them all this time and now some Montreal policeman comes to town and *you* come home to tell the world about this new thing you've discovered. Charlie, you are the bloody limit.' She walked past him up to bed.

After a while Salter had found enough justification to stop feeling horrible. Surely no one had mentioned horses around the Montagu home for years? (Right, but only out of politeness to him.) Certainly no one had taken the trouble to explain the sport to him lately. (No, not in the face of his "I-don't-want-to-know" attitude.) The truth was that harness-racing was only one, if the most outrageous, example of Salter's attitude to the whole Montagu world when he was there. From the beginning, he had defended himself against feeling like the poor cousin by refusing to get involved in activities such as sailing, playing bridge, tennis, trout-fishing with flies, and constructing bonfires suitable for baking clams. Apart from the skills involved, he was sure he would get the costume wrong, and appear in sandals for some activity that required hiking boots or bare feet. So when he was on the Island he played golf, a game he had been introduced to by some police pals; he swam; and he watched the other activities from a distance, or ignored them altogether. Over the years his bloody-mindedness and their consideration for his feelings had created two worlds, one which involved him, and the other one which they talked about and enjoyed among themselves. It was an arrangement that suited him, preserved his independence, as he put it to himself, and he took the same attitude in Toronto to his wife's interest in and understanding of art, horticulture, and science fiction. Salter came by his attitudes honestly enough; his father had tried no new foods, at home or in restaurants, for thirty years, on the grounds that it was all foreign muck and you couldn't tell what you were eating. The truth was that the old man was afraid he would make a fool of himself by not knowing how to eat it.

Salter's attitude had its dangers, and the chief one was just being demonstrated to him. He could never be sure, when he did entertain a new enthusiasm, that his wife hadn't tried to interest him in it ten years before. Science fiction was forbidden to him because she had been recommending it for so long that he had no idea who were her favourite authors. He once knew that science fiction would bore him, and now that he was not so sure, it was too late.

But harness-racing. Jesus Christ! Gradually Salter recalled bits and pieces of things he had seen or heard and ignored over the years until he became fairly sure of the truth: that harness-racing was the major maritime pastime, and that the Montagus figured prominently in the sport. Oh shit, he thought. For another half an hour he swung between justification and guilt, until he went to bed in a mood of truculent misery.

CHAPTER 2

The following morning Salter phoned the chairman of the English Department at Douglas College and arranged for some interviews. He had often seen the college as he walked downtown from his office, and he had a vague impression of two or three converted warehouses, several shiny glass buildings, and a fountain. He established that the English Department was in one of the glass boxes, and set off from his office with plenty of time to walk. He wanted to have a look at the sleazy section of Yonge Street (his favourite stretch) to see what might be 'cleaned up' for the visiting Mayor of Amsterdam. What am I supposed to do, he wondered, as he viewed the morning sprinkling of bums, homeless adolescents and strained-looking gays who called this strip home. Should I get a couple of hundred off-duty cops to walk their wives up and down, like good Toronto burghers? What the hell does 'clean up' mean? It would be easy enough to avoid the issue and drive the Mayor round the Yorkville area where, he had read in the paper, Toronto's beautiful people gathered to be looked at, but the Mayor had specifically asked to see Yonge Street because it was the only street he had heard of. Salter made a mental note to recommend that the Mayor be taken through at the lunch-hour when the street would be crowded with office workers.

The buildings of Douglas College appeared earlier than he had expected, now that he was looking for them, and Salter became aware that the College was much larger than he had thought. It was a quiet time of the academic year, between examinations and convocation, and there was only a handful of students about. The first three he asked had no idea where the English Department was, but finally he stopped one who directed him to the right building. Salter struggled through a pair of glass doors apparently designed to guard the entrance to a tomb, and found himself in the typical lobby of an academic building at the end of term. Every wall was covered with posters advertising last week's concerts, lectures, dances and the monthly meetings of the Tae Kwon Do club. It looked like the day after the Boxing Day sale.

At one side of the lobby a security guard was talking to a small plastic box held up to his mouth. Salter had to wait for him to finish his chat, evidently with a colleague at another desk somewhere, about the need to make sure someone called Wong did his share of the work. 'I said to Teperman last week, how come Wong's always on days, and me and Eddie do nights? He said, Wong's wife is up the spout, he said. He's gotta stay home nights. I said, How do you know my old lady ain't up the spout, too? Or Eddie's. You know what he said? He said, You ain't married, he said. I said, You don't have to be married, not to get someone up the spout, I said. It's all right to live common-law these days. He said, Are you? I said, No, but I could be couldn't I? You never asked me, but you believe anything that fucking Wong tells you. He does, Eddie. Sure. Anything Wong wants, and there's you and me left sucking the hind tit. You know?' Listening to this, Salter wondered again at the thousands of security guards that had sprung up in Toronto in the last ten years. Was there a job for him in the business if he ever got totally fed up with errand work? Eventually the guard noticed him, and broke off from Eddie long enough to direct him to an elevator. He rode up to the fourth floor and stepped out into an empty corridor. More notice-boards, but this time most of the announcements were about literary events and plays that had taken place during the term. One small typed notice advertised a 'complete set of texts for English 022 for sale, never been opened'. Another huge poster, printed black on a grey background said, without explanation, 'THE DEADLINE HAS BEEN CHANGED. IT IS NOW THE 28TH.' Underneath, in pencil, someone had written, 'Somehow, I still feel uneasy.'

Salter looked along the corridors which led away from the elevator at right-angles, one to the left and one straight ahead, wondering which route to take. Both looked as though they had been trashed during the night. Piles of dirty paper lay everywhere, concentrated in heaps around the office doors, but strewn along the walls as well. Some of it had been roughly gathered into cardboard boxes stacked side by side, evidently a first attempt at a clean-up. Salter's eyes cleared, and he recognized the papers as English essays, waiting to be picked up by the students, but his initial impression, that he had stumbled into an alleyway where the department threw its garbage, remained.

He chose the corridor to the left, and walked along it reading the names on the doors. As he turned the corner he almost stumbled over a girl seated at a desk, typing, and he asked directions to the chairman's office. She pointed to a corner office, the only one Salter had seen so far with the door open. There a secretary led him to the door of an inner office which opened as they approached it, and a large smiling man waved him in.

Hector Browne, the chairman of the English Department at Douglas College, was a fat dandy. Salter guessed his weight at two hundred and ten pounds, but there was nothing of the slob about him. His blue suede jacket, grey flannel trousers, and brilliant dark loafers were immaculate, and the toffee-coloured shirt made of some kind of thick linen, worn open at the neck, completed the impression of a carefully planned appearance. Salter found the total effect very pleasant, like stepping into a well-kept drawing-room. Because the building was new, Browne's office was the usual concrete and glass cube, but Browne had done his best to warm it up with some blown-up photographs of portraits that looked slightly familiar.

The chairman led him to a settee and sat down with him. 'It's about Summers, of course, Inspector?' he offered.

'Yes. Just some enquiries about what he was doing in Montreal, and who was with him.'

'It's shaken us up here, I can tell you. I wasn't close to David myself, but no man is an island, is he? Interesting how the clichés come into their own on the big occasions, isn't it?'

'Yes,' Salter said, 'If you weren't close to him—

Professor? . . . Mister? . . . What should I call you . . .
Chairman?'

'No, no, not "Chairman". It sounds like the head of the
party, doesn't it? "Mister" is fine. I *am* a professor, but so
is everyone else around here, so we don't use the title
much except on passports and that sort of thing. It's a
great help in getting through the Luxembourg Customs.
For hotel reservations, though, "Doctor" is better, if you
are a doctor, as Stephen Leacock pointed out. Ideally, of
course, one should have an arresting name—like
Rockefeller.'

'Summers was a professor?'

'We all are, as I said. Do you know anything about
Douglas College, Inspector?'

'Nothing, sir. Perhaps you could fill me in.'

Browne leaned back and put the tips of his fingers
together, parodying the gesture. He began in a lecturing
style, with enough exaggeration to show he was not to be
taken too seriously. As he talked, though, it was evident
that, rehearsed as he was, he believed what he was saying.

'Douglas College,' he said, 'was set up in the 'sixties in
response to the explosion in the demand for higher
education, a demand which the voters, as the politicians
read them, wanted satisfied. For a brief period, unique in
Ontario history—in my time, anyway—education was
politically fashionable. It was a period when Ontario
politicians anxious for higher office sought the Education
portfolio as having a very high profile, one of the largest
budgets and plenty of opportunity for headlines. During
this time the curriculum of the secondary schools was
entirely remade—destroyed, some would say—as the
trendy word went out that schools should no longer teach
subjects, but students. Schools became people-oriented.
Do you have children, Inspector?'

'I have two boys, Mr Browne, but they go to a private
school.'

'A cop-out, if I may make a play on words, Inspector.
You've never had to deal with the system. However, let
me go on. All the subjects were revamped: in English,
Creative Writing replaced the study of grammar; in the
universities, the explosion in the student population
coincided with the activist movement and the students
demanded the right to study what they liked. This was
instantly granted, as were all other student demands. But
back to numbers. To satisfy the hordes of potential voters
demanding access to higher education, or *further*
education as it was more and more called, dozens of new
colleges and quasi-colleges were created, granting new
kinds of degrees, diplomas and certificates in a variety
of new 'disciplines', such as Photographic Arts,
Horsemanship, and Gardening. The older universities
welcomed these new institutions at first. As one professor
at our rival across the street—' Browne pointed an
elaborate finger in the direction he meant '—said to me
at the time I took this job, "We are hoping you will take
all the students we don't want." But inevitably the baby
boom died down and all of the institutions of further
education, new and old, started scrambling for students.
The older institutions got frightened, for many of the
students of the next generation actually chose us even
though they would have been welcome across the street.
The establishment rushed to protect itself. First, they
lowered their entrance standards, though they will deny
this violently, then they organized to prevent the upstarts
from offering any further competition with their own
programmes. But it was too late. In the struggle that
followed some of the new institutions did suffer, but most
survived and a few prospered. Their enrolment increased,
against the trend, and in some areas they became
established as the equal of their older sister institutions.
They became, in a word, respectable.

'Douglas College—to come to my subject—is an

outstanding example. We were among the first of the new colleges, and we were blessed by an ambitious president, a downtown location, and enough time to get our feet under the table before anyone noticed. We now have ten thousand students, some programmes which take only one of four qualified applicants, our own degrees, a faculty club, and an alumni association. And we have professors with tenure, of whom David Summers was one.'

Browne was finished. Salter felt like clapping, but he had work to do. 'Thank you,' he said. 'Now about Professor Summers. If you weren't close to him, who was?'

Browne threw all his limbs into the air and arranged himself in thought. 'Good question. Pollock, of course. After that, two of the people he was in Montreal with—Carrier and Usher, and, oh yes, Marika, Marika Tils. They were all together the evening before.'

'And his enemies?'

'No one who would *kill* him, Inspector. Just academic squabbles.'

'I didn't expect you to give me the name of the killer, Professor—sorry, Mister—Browne. But an enemy might tell me something a friend would not see.'

'You can tell a man by his friends, but his enemies can save you the trouble, eh, Inspector? There are a few people who resented David. I didn't *warm* to him myself, although lately he's been more relaxed, more fun to be with.'

'Does anyone *detest* him?'

'This conversation is entirely confidential? Then Dunkley is your man. He was in Montreal, too. They couldn't *bear* each other. There was an *ancient coolness* between them, so that you would never put them on the same committee. They got on each others tits.' Browne leaned forward, smiling roundly, as he descended into argot.

'This *ancient coolness*. What was it about?'

'It started before my time. I've been here ten years, but Summers and Dunkley and several others go back twenty. Back then, those two were on opposite sides of the fence on some issue and they never forgave each other. I've heard it talked of often enough but I've never got to the bottom of it. I doubt if anyone could tell you now what happened, if anything did. It's like a neighbour thing that turns into a feud. So we kept them apart and the two of them never mentioned each other, even to their cronies. It was as if they knew some dreadful secret that kept them apart while it linked them in silent bondage, if you know what I mean. Like a theme for a Conrad story.' Browne pointed to one of the huge portraits, that of a bearded, middle-aged man.

'Conrad?'

'Joseph Conrad, the novelist, Inspector. That's his picture.'

'I know who Joseph Conrad is, Mr Browne. I meant *which* Conrad story. I've read some.' One, anyway, about someone on a boat.

'Have you? Not too many, I hope. They have a very bad effect. No. I meant it was *like* a Conrad story. One thought of Marlow and Kurtz, or "The Secret Sharer" — one of those "he - and - I - shared - a - knowledge - that - was - never - to - be - divulged - between - us" themes.'

'I see. A story Conrad never wrote.'

'No, no. The one he wrote *interminably*. Please don't take me too literally. I doubt the presence of a ghastly secret. One just thinks in these ways after years of trying to find useful analogies for first-year students.'

The phone rang and Browne answered it. 'Yes, my dear. I hadn't forgotten. Yes, my dear. I'll buy one at the Cakemaster.' He put the phone down. 'My wife,' he said. 'Reminding me that it is my daughter's birthday. I have to buy the cake. You thought I was a bachelor? I *wallow* in uxorious delight, Inspector. I have six daughters, one better than Mr Bennet. You assumed I was a bachelor because I still polish my shoes? It is possible to maintain one's standards within the nuptial bonds, you know. Conrad taught me that.' Browne was having a wonderful time.

Salter said, 'Nothing surprises me any more, Mr Browne. See? Another cliché. Now, where can I find these people? Carrier or Usher first, I think.'

'They are waiting for you. I've arranged interviews with everyone who was with David in Montreal. They are upset, but you are used to that I expect. Marika is in *misery.*'

'And his buddy, — Hillock?'

'Pollock. He's here, too.' Browne stood up with a little jump and started to bustle. 'Now I can't ask you for lunch because I always bring my own.'

'Diet, sir?' Salter asked rudely, curious to know what kept this shining beauty in trim.

'Wrong again. I like myself the way I am. So does my wife. See?' He opened the brown paper bag. Inside were four jelly doughnuts and a pint of chocolate milk. 'I pick them up on the way to work and I look forward to them all morning. I'm in my office all the time if you need me.'

'Will you be at the funeral?'

'Yes. Will you be there?'

'I expect so, sir. The killer always turns up, doesn't he? I read that somewhere.'

'Ha, ha, ha. I get it. Another cliché.'

'Would you keep our conversation confidential, sir? And try to stop any speculation around the office.'

'Mum's the word, Inspector. Good luck.' He looked forlorn for a moment. 'I hope it turns out to be a passing thug and not someone we know.' His voice was quavering slightly. Through the sparkle, Browne was keeping the horror at bay.

'It usually does, sir,' Salter said, resisting a mild impulse to give Browne a pat. 'Goodbye.'

Carrier was next. He sat behind his desk without speaking as Salter sat down in a chair opposite him. A tidy man in his early forties with fair, thinning hair, he was wearing a neat checked sports shirt and khaki trousers. He had his own teapot and cup beside him on a little table, and a packet of Peek Frean's biscuits. On the wall, three posters under glass gave the appearance of a matched set, although their subjects didn't seem connected as far as Salter could see. One was a portrait of a delicate young man with lace around his wrists, probably Shelley or someone; the second was a reproduction of a lot of writing—a page from the oldest book in the world? The third picture looked familiar, being an advertisement of an art gallery exhibit with a reproduction of a picture of a red checked tablecloth. What luck, Salter thought, as he recognized the only Canadian painting he had ever looked at closely. The original belonged to some cultured friends of his wife, and Salter had frequently studied it and failed to find any reason for its artistic and (huge) monetary worth. He introduced himself and pointed to the poster.

'Have you followed de Niverville's career, Dr Carrier?' he asked, one connoisseur to another.

'Yes,' Carrier said.

'Interesting painter,' Salter said, trying to remember a single fact about him.

'Yes,' Carrier said.

So much for art, the key that opens all doors, thought Salter. 'Now, sir,' he said, 'I want to ask you a few questions about Professor Summers. First, I'd like you to tell me what happened when you were all together on Thursday. You were with Professor Summers for dinner, I think. Who else was there?'

'Usher, Dunkley, Marika Tils and I. That's all. Nothing happened. We just had dinner.'

'Wasn't it unusual, Professor, for Summers and Dunkley to be having dinner together?'

'Yes.'

There was a long pause.

'Well?' Salter asked.

'Yes, it was unusual.'

'Then why were they together?'

'We all were.'

'So you say. But normally Dunkley and Summers avoided each other.'

'Yes.'

'But not this time.'

'No.'

Jesus Christ. 'Mr Carrier. I'm trying to find out who killed a man. I'd be glad of any help. Could you tell me, please, why, on this particular night these two old enemies were together?'

'Summers invited him along with the rest of us.'

'Ah. Why?' Could you perhaps offer an interpretation? Rack your trained, scholarly brain, Salter thought.

'He said that tonight was his night. He said the gods were smiling on him. So he insisted we all go out to dinner. Including Dunkley.'

'What did he mean by "The gods were smiling"?'

'I don't know.'

'He never said?'

'No. He just seemed very happy.'

'I see. He just said, "The gods are smiling; this is on me"?'

'I don't remember exactly what he said. We were all having a drink in a bar after the last paper.'

'All of you, including Dunkley?'

'Yes. He had just read a paper.'

'Read a paper?'

'Yes. On favourite epithets in John Clare's poetry.'

'I see. Read it to other people, you mean. Lectured, like.'

'Yes.'

'And then Summers issued his invitation.'

'Yes.'

'And no one asked what it was all about?'

'Oh yes. We all asked him. But he wouldn't tell us. He said he would tell us later.'

'A good dinner?' Salter knew the answer but was curious to know how long it would take him to get this bugger to tell it.

'I beg your pardon?'

'Did he give you a good dinner?' That seem clear, sir?

'Yes. We went to the Maison Victor Hugo. I can't remember what I had but it was very good.'

'Did you notice the bill?'

'Yes.'

In a minute, thought Salter, I am going to take this loquacious bastard back to the office and stick the Oldest Sergeant on the Force on to him. Gatenby would enjoy asking him the four hundred niggling questions he calls interrogation, and with this one it might work. Aloud he said, 'How much was it?'

'I don't know exactly.'

'Roughly. Give me a round figure.'

'About a hundred and thirty dollars. Plus the tip, of course.'

'Cash or card?' asked Salter, who had already seen the charge slip.

'He used a Visa card.'

'And then what?'

'After a while we went back to our rooms.'

'Where did you go first?'

'Marika went back to her hotel right away. About nine o'clock. Then we walked about a bit. Then Summers left.

Then the three of us went for one more drink. Then we walked to the hotel.'

'You were all staying at the same hotel?'

'Yes. The Hotel Esmeralda.'

'But Summers was staying at the Hotel Plaza del Oro or some such name?'

'Yes. But the rest of us were at the Esmeralda.'

'And you all went back to bed.'

'Yes.'

'And you didn't see or hear anything of each other, until breakfast the next morning?'

'I saw Dunkley, of course.'

'Why, "of course"?'

'We shared a room.'

'I see. That's wonderful. You two have alibis.'

'I think that is a ridiculous and extremely unpleasant remark, Inspector,' Carrier said, flaring up in a temper.

'True, though, isn't it? And Usher?'

'He shared a room with a friend of his from another university.'

'And Miss Tils?'

'She was on her own.'

'I see. Well, that seems to be everything you know, doesn't it? One or two more points. Were you all drunk?'

'Drunk?'

'Smashed. Loaded. Pissed. I don't know the academic term.'

'We had a lot of wine. But I wasn't drunk.' Carrier was still simmering.

'Who was?'

'Summers drank a lot more than the rest of us. He was stumbling a little.'

'Finally, then, you know of no reason why Summers should have been celebrating?'

'I had the impression that more than one thing was contributing to his state. "Everything's coming up roses" was what he said once.'

'Might there have been a woman involved?'

'What do you mean?'

'Could he have been in love, say?'

'I don't see why that should have made him buy us all dinner.'

Salter sighed. 'Nor do I. But middle-aged men, men of our age, Professor, do funny things, I hear. Thank you. Don't go out of town without telling me, will you? And don't talk about this case to anyone, especially the people you were with on Friday night.'

'Am I under suspicion, Inspector?'

'At this stage, Professor, we try to keep an open mind.

Salter walked down the corridor until he found Usher's office, wondering if all the interviewees would be as tight-arsed. His initial sight of Usher cheered him up. The door was opened by a swarthy little man so covered in hair that only his forehead and nose showed through.

'Come in, come in, Inspector. Here we go. Sit down here. Cup of tea? If this was Oxford we could have sherry, but here we have to make do.'

Usher was a shouter. His voice was as noisy as a television set tuned for the deaf. His accent was English working class, not quite cockney, for all his aitches were stressed heavily, but otherwise it was classically what the English call 'common'. As he made Salter comfortable, he moved about the office in giant loping strides that kept him close to the ground; he put a chair in place, settled an ashtray, cleared a space for Salter to write on, and finally seated himself behind his desk, all the while shouting and smiling through his beard, an enormous crescent of yellow teeth splitting his face like a half-moon.

'You all right now, Inspector? That sun bother you? Move your chair a bit over there. Go on. That's it. You want something to write on? Take my statement? Har,

har. No. You all right, really? Off we go, then.'

When he had subsided, Salter asked, 'Professor Usher?'

'Yes, that's right. The name's on the door. Smoke?
Don't mind me. I don't. My kids won't let me. Har, har.
Terrible'n't? I don't mind if you do, though. It won't
come this way. No. I suppose you chaps are givin' it up
like everybody else. Funny how it's changed. I used to
smoke forty a day once.'

Usher did a comic cough, and Salter shot through the
tiny gap. 'I wonder if you would corroborate your
colleagues' story of the events of Friday night.'

'Glad to. Glad to. We met in the bar about half past
five, had a drink and left about a quarter past six. P'raps
twenty past. No. I'm tellin' a lie. It was *half* past six 'cause
they were closing the bar up, you see.'

'I've got the main story, I think,' Salter shouted. 'Just
one or two details. First of all, would you say Summers
was drunk?'

'Drunk as a fart, Inspector. I've seen some people lap it
up, but *him*! I thought we'd have to put him to bed. You
think that's what did it? Someone saw him, followed him
home? Seems likely, doesn't it? Rotten, really. He was
having such a good time, too. I must say . . .'

Salter attacked again. 'Why?' he bellowed. 'Why was
he having such a good time. Did he say?'

'No. He went on all night about the gods smilin', but he
never told us why.'

'After he left you, you and Dunkley and Carrier stayed
in the area for a while and had a few more drinks, right?'

'Old Carrier tell you that? You could call it that. Not
quite true, though. He's a bit shy, is Carrier. No, we went
back to *one* place and had a nightcap, if you like. More of
an eye-opener, really.' Usher imitated a man looking
through binoculars, and waited to be asked what he was
up to. Salter waited in turn. Usher continued.

'Place called "Les Jardins du Paradis"—French place.

More like the Black Hole.'

'A bar?'

'Yerss. A bar. With gels. Strippers. Continuous live performance. Take it off, take it off, all the customers cried, and they did, right on the table.' Usher roared with laughter.

'You went *back* to this place. You had already gone there with Summers.'

'Yerss. Soon as Marika went home, old Dave started talking about finding the action. So he asked a policeman — that's what you do in Montreal — and he told us about these two bars. One of them wasn't much, but this second one, the Jardins place, was full of lovely crumpet. We had a real basinful.'

'A basinful wasn't enough, though. After Summers left, you went back.'

'That's right. Soldiers on leave, we were.'

'Then you all went back to the hotel. Did you stay in your room that night? I have to ask that.'

' 'Course you do. No. I didn't sneak out and do in old Dave. You can check up with my mate from New Brunswick, if you like. He was in the room when I got back and we were up half the night, talking.'

'You stayed with a friend from New Brunswick?'

'That's right, Inspector. That's the nice thing about these conferences. You get a chance to meet old pals.'

'Is that the main purpose, Professor?'

'Now, now, now, Inspector. Don't *you* start. A little conference once a year is the only perks we get. No. It's not the *main* purpose. The main purpose is to refresh us academically.' Usher gave a low-comedy wink. 'But it's one of the nice things about them. We all move around a bit in this game, first in graduate school, then usually a couple of jobs while we're finishing the thesis, and these conferences bring together everybody you've met. Actually it *is* a little outing for us. You see a different

place every year. Last year we all went to
Moncton—smashing lobsters there—and the year before
that was Saskatoon. Only a couple of us went there.'
Usher roared with laughter. 'Saskatoon, Saskatchewan,'
he said derisively. 'The year before that it was Edmonton.
That turned out all right because of the Hot Springs at
Jasper. Lovely, they are. Next year we go to Halifax.
There will be a line-up for that one, I can tell you. The
maritimes conferences are always popular. Except
Newfoundland.'

'Kind of a convention, is it? Like the Kiwanis?'

'Now you're being a bit sarcastic, I can tell. Still, fair's
fair. We do some work, of course, but the main thing is
getting away in a gang.'

'And is that how you go? All of you, in a gang?'

'If we can. Of course, we're not all as thick as thieves
when we are at home, but at the conferences we do stick
together, yes.'

'You travel down and back together?'

'We did this time. Marika and John Carrier and me.
We went down in my car. Dunkley always goes on his
own.'

'Why?'

'Who knows? He just does. But so did old Dave. He
always went on his own, too.'

'Why?'

'Search me. There was room in my car, but he went
down by train. Did the same thing last year. And he
always stays in a different hotel from the rest of us. I used
to think it was just chance, but I watched him this year,
out of curiosity. Sure enough, he dawdled about when we
were trying to make our arrangements, putting us off
when we were trying to double up in rooms, to cut down
the cost; then, when we'd all booked, he reserved at
another hotel. I realized then that he always does that. I
still don't think there's anything in it, though. I'll tell you

why. When we were in Moncton last year, he always turned up late at the parties they have in the evenings. A bit mysterious, you'd think? So would I. But you know where he'd been? At the races. They have harness-racing at Moncton, and he snuck off every night to play the gee-gees. Someone saw him there. Sly bugger. But I think he was just shy about telling us. Not very academic, is it?'

Usher had quietened down slightly as he grew reflective, and showed signs of stopping altogether. Salter thought he would never have a chance to hear about Summers from someone with as little bias as Usher, and he prodded him on.

'So you don't think it was unusual for Summers to be in a room to himself in another hotel from the rest of you?'

'As I say, I did once. But he always stayed on his own, didn't he? Every year.'

'So. At night he went to the races. What about during the day?'

'He heard a few papers, like the rest of us. Not all day, of course, and not the same ones.'

'There are different discussions going on at the same time?'

'Oh yes. There were four sessions a day, and five or six different papers at each session. In different rooms, of course. There are always a couple of important sessions, given by the big-wigs, and everyone goes to them, but generally, for the small ones, we all go to different ones and meet afterwards.'

'Did you see Summers at any of the papers?'

'There was only time for one session, wasn't there, and Dunkley was giving one of the papers. I didn't go to it, and I don't think anyone else did, either. Even David didn't go, and it was in his field.'

'What field is that?'

'Romantic poetry. Wordsworth was all David cared about.'

'He should have gone, then, to Dunkley's paper?'

Usher looked unhappy at seeming to criticize a colleague. 'Yes, he should have,' he agreed.

'Dunkley and Summers both taught Romantic poetry, did they?'

'No. That was the trouble.' Usher looked even more miserable. He consulted his watch. 'Here. Inspector. What about a bite. Let's go and have a sandwich and a bowl of suds and I will fill you in. It's all bullshit, really, but you might as well know it.'

Salter agreed, and Usher loped around the room, collecting his jacket and tidying his papers. 'I'll take you to the Faculty Club,' he said. 'Give you an insight into life at Douglas College.' Usher roared with laughter again.

'You know the college, Inspector?' he asked as they were descending in the elevator.

'I've walked past it dozens of times and your chairman told me the history. Why?'

They left the building and paused on the steps. 'We are now in the Arts Building,' Usher began. 'Over there is the Administration Building, the great big shiny one. That there is the library, and all those old houses contain the other departments. This is called the quad.' Usher pointed to the square of grass in front of them. 'We are going over there.' He started off across the grass in an outdoor version of the giant steps he used in the office. Salter was hard put to keep up without trotting as they raced across the tiny quadrangle.

'Here we are, then,' Usher said, leading Salter into the front door of a renovated old brick house. 'The Faculty Club—among other things.'

Inside a little hallway they hung their coats on a peg and moved into the dining-room, a pleasant, sunny little room furnished like a superior hotel coffee-shop.

'Mr Usher!' the waiter shouted, as soon as they were inside. 'How did I do, sir?'

'Bombed, laddie, bombed. Absolutely buggered,' Usher shouted back, grinning at the student. 'Good thing you've got a job here, but judging by your English exam, you must have trouble reading the menu. I have never come across such a load of unadulterated, illiterate twaddle in all my born days. And what did you use for a pen? Your handwriting, laddie, looks like the death-throes of a mad chicken who's just run through a puddle of ink.'

The waiter accepted all this with a grin, and asked again, 'How did I do?'

'You passed, laddie, you passed. Now get us two draught and I'll give you an "A".'

To Salter's relief, the horseplay now seemed at an end, and the waiter led them to a table. Usher looked round the room, waved at a couple of people, called greetings to another, and the beer arrived. Salter was beginning to be sorry he had accepted Usher's invitation. How was he going to question the man with a dozen people listening? He hoped his host had a confidential voice, but as soon as they were settled Usher picked up the story again in the same penetrating tones. Most of the conversation in the dining-room stopped as the other diners listened.

'The thing you've got to understand, Inspector,' Usher said, causing Salter to hope the others would take him for an inspector of drains, 'is that we all have a field. What we specialize in. My field is Lawrence. D.H. I come from Nottingham — did you realize I'm English? — and my grandfather knew Lawrence, or said he did, like most of the old codgers in Nottingham.' Usher broke off again for a sustained maniacal laugh at the lies Nottingham codgers told about Lawrence. 'Anyway, he had a lot of stories about Bert, so when I went into English, Lawrence seemed a natural to specialize in. Our chairman is a Conrad man, Carrier is working on Tennyson, and Dunkley and old Dave are Romantics. That's the trouble.

You see, we don't have many students, only about twenty in Honours English, and we don't have enough of any kind of students for two sections of anything—do you follow me?—and Dave taught our only Romantics course. He had seniority, and until he went on sabbatical, Dunkley wouldn't get a look-in.'

'When would that be? Summers's sabbatical?' Salter spoke so quietly that he could feel the other diners straining to hear.

'Year after next, I think.'

'I see. So, in a sense, Summers had Dunkley's course, until then.'

'I suppose so. But talking about "your" course or "my" course just leads to a lot of bad feeling, and there was enough of that.'

Their sandwiches arrived, and Salter took the opportunity to change the subject. He asked Usher questions about how hard he worked, how much professors were paid, and what the pressures were on a teacher of English at Douglas College, all designed to look like part of his investigation into the causes of Summers's death, and he got for his pains a lengthy speech on the teacher's life as Usher saw it, which ended with the information that Usher, personally, was delighted to be paid well for doing something he enjoyed and would do for much less if he had to.

'But not everyone feels like you do, eh?' Salter asked.

'There are just as many teachers who shouldn't be doing it as there are policemen, I expect,' Usher said. And then, 'Not us, though, by God. Not you and me, Inspector,' and he roared with glee again.

They walked back to the Arts Building together. When they reached the door, Usher put out his hand. 'I've got some errands to do, Inspector. I might see you later. I wasn't all that pally with David. Didn't know him well at all, but I was one of the last to see him alive.' Usher for

the first time was speaking quietly. 'It's like the Venerable
Bede said—in one window and out the other—that's life.'
He turned away and walked off down the street.

Back in the English Department, Salter had plenty of
time before he was scheduled to meet Dunkley, the next
on his list, and he got the secretary to let him into
Summers's office, which had been locked since his death.

A small room, furnished with two chairs and a desk,
like all the others. On the wall, four or five mounted but
unframed photographs, more artistic than realistic to
Salter's eye (one of them was so out of focus it must have
been intentional). Four shelves of books: on one shelf the
books were interleaved with notes; all the other books
looked like old texts or publishers' free samples. Salter
opened a desk drawer; it was full of rubbish—overshoes, a
coffee-pot, and a clock with a broken face. He opened the
other drawers, and found a few personal-looking letters
which he began to read. The door opened and a young
man poked his head round it.

'Dave in?' he asked.

Salter shook his head.

'Know when he'll be back?'

Salter shrugged, dodging. 'Why? Who wants him?'

'I do. He's got my essay.'

'You a student?'

'That's right. Theatre Arts. Dave teaches us Modern
Drama. Oh well.' The head disappeared.

Dave? A palsy-walsy teacher? Or was that standard
these days? Salter continued reading the dead man's mail
without much interest. A letter from a friend in England.
Two others from former students.

The door opened again and another student stood in
the doorway.

'Professor Summers?' he asked.

'No.'

'You're not Professor Summers?'

'No. What do you want him for?'

'I was told to see him. By my chairman. Professor Summers is my English teacher.'

'And you don't know what he looks like?'

'I'm in Journalism. We're pretty busy. Not too much time for English. I haven't had a chance to check out what's going on this term. Oh well. I'll come back later.' He disappeared.

Salter finished turning over Summers's desk and leafed through his desk diary—looking for what? Before he could answer that to himself, the secretary appeared to tell him that Dunkley was waiting in his office.

'I didn't like Summers, as you have no doubt been told.' Dunkley sat behind his desk, being interviewed. A handsome man; tall, thick fair hair to his shoulders, slightly balding in front. A still upright carriage. He was wearing army surplus clothing which he seemed to invest with its original military purpose. His office was lined with notices of meetings concerning aid to various refugee groups. Like most of his colleagues that Salter had seen, Dunkley was about forty.

'I've heard as much. But no one has told me why.'

'Because they don't know. It has nothing to do with them. Or you, either.'

'It might, you know. You've been feuding for ten years, I hear. Might be reason enough to kill him.'

'You are not paid to joke with suspects, are you, Inspector?'

'Perhaps you could fill me in on what I am paid for, Professor?'

'Persecution, mainly, of people who can't defend themselves, as far as I can tell.'

'Fascist pigs, are we?'

'Could you come to the point?'

'All right. Why were you feuding?'

'There was no feud.'

'Just you hating him and him hating you, for ten years.'

'We disliked each other. Can we get on, please? I am extremely busy.' The diction was precise, but underneath the vowels were flat.

'You are Australian, Mr Dunkley?'

'I was born in New Zealand. My family was German, originally. They changed their name from Dunkel in 1939 for patriotic reasons. I am married but separated from my wife, whom I still support. What else?'

'It's Summers I want to find out about. What did you have against him?'

'I detested him. In my opinion, he should not have been teaching here?'

'Why? Did he fuck the students?'

'Probably. I was more concerned with his academic standards.'

'Poor, were they, in your opinion?'

'Non-existent.'

'Bad teacher, was he?'

'In my opinion.'

'What about the students?'

'Some of them enjoyed the kind of thing he did, no doubt.'

'Did you ever see him teach?'

'No.'

'But you heard?'

'Yes.'

'From the students.'

'Yes.'

'They complained to you, did they?'

'They rarely knew enough to complain, but from what I heard I knew what was going on.'

'I see. Were his politics very different from yours?'

'He had no politics. He was an opportunist in that area, too.'

'I see. Well, well. He sounds pretty bad. Could we get back to the Friday night in Montreal? You got over your distaste for him enough to accept his hospitality. He bought you a dinner, I believe.'

'Yes, he did. I don't know where he got the money.'

'Why did you accept his hospitality?'

'He asked me in front of the others. They knew I had no plans. So I took the easy way out.'

'For a change.'

'What?'

'You took the easier path for a change. In spite of your preference for the hard one.'

'What are you talking about, Inspector?'

'I'm not sure.' Which was true. Salter had forgotten himself in his dislike for the man he was talking to. 'So you went along,' he continued. 'When did Miss Tils leave the group?'

'After dinner. About nine.'

'Then what?'

'Then Summers took us to a striptease show.'

'Then what?'

'Summers went back to his hotel.'

'Was he drunk?'

'Sodden. At least I thought so at the time.'

'What time did he leave you?'

'About ten o'clock.'

'Why do you say "you thought so"?'

'I think he may have been play-acting.'

'Why?'

'I think he may have gone off to get a whore.'

'What makes you think that?'

'He talked about it during the show.'

'But *you* were just watching the show to keep him company?'

'I saw it differently. Those girls were being paid to cater to the likes of Summers.'

'Exploitation of minority group?'

'Yes. As a matter of fact.'

'What happened after Summers went home?'

'We had another drink and walked about a bit. Then we went back ourselves. Carrier and I went to our room. I presume Usher did, too, although I can't confirm that.'

'That's all right, Professor. I can. But this last drink. Where did you go for it?'

Now Dunkley's face went darker. 'Back to the bar,' he said. 'As you obviously know.'

'I have to confirm everything, Professor. You tell me. The same show?'

'Yes.'

'Why?'

'I don't talk behind my colleagues' backs. Ask *them*.'

'I have. They wanted to see some more tits. What was your idea? To organize a protest?'

Dunkley said nothing. Salter pressed on. 'The striptease show didn't have t e same effect on you, Professor? There was no thought of you finding a girl?'

'We went home to bed.'

'What time was that?'

'I couldn't tell you. About half past ten.'

'That's a bit early, isn't it?'

'I don't have to explain my sleeping habits to you, I think.'

'It was your regular time, then, was it? Ten-thirty?'

'Yes. And I had had a hard day.'

'Right. You read a paper that day. Get a big audience?'

'The room was half full.'

'But none of your colleagues here came.'

'None of my colleagues knew anything about my subject.'

'Summers did, didn't he? His field was the same as yours, wasn't it?'

Dunkley was silent.

'Wasn't it?'

'Summers didn't have a field.'

'I see. He thought he did, though, didn't he? Wordsworth, Keats, and such-like.'

'So I believe.'

'But you and he never discussed your fields?'

'Very few people around here talk about literature. Mostly they talk about mortgages and wine-making.'

'Sounds like our canteen. Could we get back to the night you went to bed at ten-thirty, your normal time. What time do you normally get up?'

'At six, as a matter of fact. I usually get a couple of hours' work in before breakfast.'

'So you got up at six,' Salter said, writing laboriously in his notebook. 'Carrier, too?'

'No. I *didn't* get up at six that morning. I had a very restless night, and I didn't get to sleep until the small hours. We didn't get up until after eight.'

Why is he lying, Salter wondered. Surely he and Carrier didn't do a Burke and Hare on Summers?

'I see,' he said. 'You won't mind signing a statement to that effect will you, sir?'

'Of course not.'

'Thank you, Mr Dunkley. And I'll tell you what. If you ever feel like telling me what you had against Summers, here's my number. I'll ask everybody else, anyway.'

Dunkley allowed the card to lie on his desk. He said nothing.

'Don't get up,' Salter said, rising from his chair, 'And don't leave town.'

'I am a suspect?'

'Everyone is, Professor, until we find the killer.'

Marika Tils spoke English with a thick, north European accent. What was *she* doing in an English Department?

'I am Dutch, Inspector. I learned my English as a

second language, although I have an M.A. from the University of Toronto, which is the one they all bow down to here. I compared *Paradise Lost* with a Dutch poem of the same kind. Here I teach English to foreign students, mostly Chinese from Hong Kong, although we are getting them from everywhere.' The syntax was impeccable, but the accent was so thick it sounded affected. Salter was reminded of a story he had heard once about a similar situation, and he tried to joke.

'Isn't there a danger of turning out a lot of Chinese students with Dutch accents, Miss Tils?'

She smiled. 'Not much. But if the grammar were all right, it wouldn't matter much, would it? Just an interesting problem for the local Professor Higgins.'

Good. A nice relief from Dunkley. She was a woman in her late thirties, just beginning to wrinkle slightly. Straight blonde hair, nice, slightly lumpy features and a good, if large, body. Graceful, feminine, she looked like an athlete, a swimmer or an equestrian. In the right dress, (or naked in the sun, thought Salter) she was probably breath-taking. Her one disturbing feature was that in colouring and in her carriage she seemed distantly related to Dunkley. Her complexion was splotchy, and her eyes looked sore. Someone, at last, was grieving for Summers.

'I'll come to the point, Miss Tils. Would you call yourself a friend of David Summers?'

'Oh yes. I liked him very much.'

What did that mean, translated from the Dutch?

'Does that mean you were lovers?'

'Oh no. Not in that way. But I wish we had been, now. He was happily married, and I am also not free. No, I mean I liked him. He was wonderful.'

'In what way?'

She shrugged. 'I could talk to him. I could trust him. He liked me. What else?'

'He doesn't seem to have affected everybody that way.'

'Of course not. He was *my* friend, very special to me, but I don't mean he was Jesus Christ. Lots of people didn't like him.'

'But you weren't lovers?'

'I told you, no. But that was by the way. We didn't lie down together, but I might have.' She was annoyed at Salter's interest.

'Could I ask you about the Friday evening? First, do you know why he was so happy?'

'No. But it wasn't just a mood. Something had happened, but he never got a chance to tell me in front of the others. You know about him and Dunkley?'

'I know something. What was the trouble between them?'

'I don't know. They were involved in a way that made them hate each other. Like old accomplices who were ashamed of the old days. If you want to know what I think, I think it was something stupid, like they bumped into each other in a body-rub parlour or something. Dunkley is a fanatic, of course, and he would hate anyone who caught him doing something wrong. Maybe it was politics. I don't know. You can be sure it was something not very interesting.'

'Your chairman said they were like two people in a Conrad story.'

'Yes. I've heard him say that. But Conrad was another one who made mountains out of molehills.'

'From what you and others have said, Dunkley and Summers were very different people.'

'As chalk from cheese, Inspector.'

'Does that mean you don't like Dunkley?'

'This is very—unorthodox, isn't it?'

'Yes, I suppose it is. But I'm trying to find out what kind of man Summers was, and something about the people around him. You don't have to tell me.'

'All right. No, it doesn't mean that, of course, but in answer to your real question, I don't like Dunkley, but not for any reason connected with David.'

'What then?'

'Oh, for God's sake. I don't like the way he eats. His breath is bad. I don't know. Why don't you like people? I just don't like him.'

'Sorry. Now, after dinner you went back to the hotel. Did you spend the rest of the night by yourself in your room?'

She blushed deeply. Embarrassment or anger?'

'What does that question mean?'

'I'm sorry. I put it badly. Did you leave your room for any purpose after you returned to the hotel.'

'No. Oh, I see. You mean did I kill David.' Her tone was disgusted. 'No I did not leave my room and go to David's hotel and kill him.'

'That wasn't what I meant, although you are strong enough, and you might have a motive I don't know about. We found a glass with lipstick on it in his room.'

'Ah, you think I might have gone to make love with him?' She relaxed and shook her head. 'I wish I had. He might be alive now.'

'Somebody visited him, Miss Tils. A woman.'

'Apparently, Inspector, but not me. I haven't worn lipstick in ten years.' She looked interested in spite of herself, 'I wonder who David had tucked away in Montreal?'

'I'll find out. Miss Tils, as a friend of Professor Summers, do you know anything about his private life that might lead to someone killing him? Women, debts, anything like that?'

She shook her head. 'It must be something like that, I know. But I don't know of anyone. Certainly no one here, not even Dunkley.'

'How can you be so sure?'

'He's got an alibi, hasn't he? But call it my intuition. I

know Dunkley. He wouldn't do anything like that.'

Once again the hair prickled on Salter's scalp as he felt her withholding something. What's going on, he wondered.

On an impulse, instead of meeting his last appointment immediately, he returned to Carrier's office and walked in without waiting for an invitation. As he appeared, Dunkley rose from his chair and walked past him, ignoring him. Carrier sat still, saying nothing, and Salter took the vacant chair.

'Mr Carrier. I forgot to ask you about a statement. Since you and Professor Dunkley roomed together, you will be able to confirm each other's story, won't you? I'll need a statement signed. May I just check the facts again?' Salter consulted his notebook and pretended to read back to Carrier what he had said. He continued, 'A couple more details then. What time did you and Professor Dunkley get to your room?'

'About ten-thirty.'

'And you stayed all night in your room?'

'Yes.'

'What time did you leave it in the morning?'

'I don't remember. After eight.'

'You must have been tired out. A bit drunk?'

Carrier said nothing.

'Well, that checks, doesn't it?' Salter said with a smile. 'If you can think of anything that might help me, anything at all, anything Summers said or did, for example, you'll let me know won't you? I'll check all this with the hotel staff, of course, but I don't expect they will have noticed anything, will they?'

Why are you looking so frightened, Salter wondered. Probably because you went back for a last trip to the stripjoint. Or a whorehouse. Were they legal in Montreal?

Salter stared hard at the professor, wishing he knew more about interrogation techniques.

Last came Pollock. The name sounded familiar to Salter, but the man was a stranger to him. He was the first one Salter had met who looked like a proper professor. Dark suit, large bow tie, and black, old-fashioned boots which he placed at right-angles to each other as he bowed (or seemed to) his visitor through the door. Smallish and dapper, he affected a curly pipe with a lid, held in his mouth with one hand. When Salter was inside, he turned, placed his boots at right-angles again and waited for Salter to speak.

He's trying to twinkle, Salter thought, but he's a bit young for it. About thirty-five.

Eventually, after a long puff at his pipe, Pollock went around his desk and sat down, crossing his legs sideways to the desk and propping the elbow supporting the pipe on the desk with his head facing Salter.

He's going to say, 'What can I do for you, Inspector?' thought Salter.

Pollock removed the pipe, looked at it, put it back, puffed on it, removed it again, and said, 'What can I do for you, Inspector?'

'I need a motive, Mr Pollock, and I might find it in Summers's background. I am told you were his oldest friend here. First, do you know of any women in his life, apart from his wife?' Salter felt as if he was on stage, playing 'the policeman' to Pollock's 'professor'.

Pollock considered. 'No,' he said decisively. 'There have been. But not for years.'

'You are sure of that?'

'Certain. David never had long affairs. Over the years he fell in love once or twice; I always knew, because he told me. And his wife. That's why they didn't last long.'

'His wife put a stop to them?'

'No. Just the fact that she knew.'

'But he was not "in love" at the moment?'

'No.'

'You are certain?'

'Yes.'

'There could have been no brief fling in Montreal with one of his colleagues, perhaps?' I don't usually talk like this, thought Salter wonderingly.

'No.'

'You are certain?'

'Yes.'

Now it was in danger of becoming one of those nightmares on stage where a bit of dialogue keeps returning to its departure point because of a wrong cue. Salter shook himself.

'Do you mind telling me how you are so sure of yourself?'

Pollock puffed four times and delivered his line. 'Because he only has one female colleague, Marika Tils, and he did not have a brief fling with her.'

'How do you know?'

'Because I asked her.'

'I see. And she is to be believed, is she?'

'Absolutely.' Puff, pause, puff. 'You see, Inspector,' puff, 'Marika and I are lovers.' Puff, puff, puff.

Jesus Christ, thought Salter. What a world these people live in. He pulled a scrap of paper from his pocket. 'These conversations are entirely confidential, Professor, and I think I can trust you. This message was found in his mailbox in the hotel.' He read it: 'See you later. Wait for me. Jane.'

Pollock looked confused.

Gotcha, thought Salter.

Then: 'Ah yes,' Pollock said. 'I knew all about Jane, of course. But she didn't seem to be covered by your question. Jane is Jane Homer, Dean of Women at

Wollstonecraft Hall. They were just old friends.'

'I see.' Salter made a note. 'Now, Professor, I wonder if you would mind telling me everything about Summers that might help me to understand him. If I can get an idea of what kind of man he was it might help a great deal.'

Pollock began a seminar on his dead friend. Salter pretended to take notes to give Pollock's words their proper value.

'He was, I think, a good teacher, a very fair critic, a poor scholar, and a very poor student. He worked hard at his job here — too hard, probably; he had something interesting to say about what he was teaching, but he didn't keep up with his field and he didn't produce anything. His friends thought he failed to apply his talents, and his enemies accused him of having a butterfly mind. I think myself he had reached the age when it is now fashionable to change careers. The symptoms were that he had become involved in a whole host of activities in the last year or two that one could only see as distractions.'

'Like?'

'Like squash, Inspector. He took up squash last year, and played it four or five times a week. It was the high point of his day.'

'Was he good?'

'No. I played him after he had been playing for a year. He was no good at all. But among the people he played down at that club of his, he was able to find keen competition.'

'What else?'

'Making money. Obviously, he had decided to try and make his fortune. He was always a bit of a gambler — poker, the races — that sort of thing — he bought every lottery ticket going — and lately he was dabbling in commodities.

'Did he break out in any other ways?'

'You want to know if he was having a "mid-life crisis"? I think that's the jargon. Perhaps. He didn't start to dress like a gypsy, though, or wear a wig, or any of the other symptoms I've heard about. No, if I understand the mid-life crisis, it is an attempt to have a few more years of boyhood in middle age, at least that's how it manifests itself around here. Well, perhaps that's what he was doing, but in his case the symptoms were a sudden renewed interest in games and in taking risks.'

'Who were his friends, Professor?'

'Me, of course, and Marika. One or two others in the department enjoyed his company. Otherwise the people he and his wife socialized with. He didn't have many friends, the way people use that term nowadays, but he tended to keep them.'

'His enemies?'

'A lot of people were wary of him. He had a bad habit of looking for the funny side of any situation, and sometimes he was witty at the expense of others. He teased people and they took offence. And teasing *is* a form of cruelty, isn't it?'

'I'm trying to understand the relationship between him and Dunkley,' Salter said, coming to the point. 'Can you help me there?'

'Yes. I thought we'd come to that. You've heard Browne's theory, no doubt, of a Conradian link?'

'Yes. You think it makes sense?'

'Oh, it makes sense, Inspector, but it would be more impressive if someone else had put it forward. Coming from Browne, it doesn't carry much weight. Browne did his thesis on Conrad. That is the only author he knows.'

'You don't think much of it, then.'

'Not really. I think they just struck sparks off each other.'

'Summers never confided in you—about his feelings for

Dunkley, and the reasons?'

'No, he didn't. That's why I don't think there's any mystery. He would certainly have said something to me. We were very close.' And then, quite unexpectedly, Pollock stopped acting, and his eyes filled with tears. He put his pipe down, and blew his nose.

Salter gave him a few moments by pretending to scribble. Then he said, gently enough, 'It does seem strange, though, that he never discussed such a well-known feud with you, sir, his closest friend?'

But Pollock was now too upset to speculate with him. He shrugged and fiddled with the relighting of his pipe.

Salter put his notebook away and stood up. 'If anything occurs to you that you think I might find helpful, you can find me at the Headquarters building. Thank you very much, sir.' He left the professor still blinking at his pipe.

As he walked down the corridor he heard someone behind him, and he slowed down enough at the corner to see Marika Tils go into Pollock's office.

CHAPTER 3

'What would make two guys not speak to each other for ten years?' Salter asked. They were sitting at the back of their house on a concrete slab, looking at the grass. Their neighbours would have called it having coffee on the patio in the garden, but from motives of inverted snobbery, though different in each case, Salter and Annie referred to the area as 'the yard'. Salter had been raised in Cabbagetown, and 'the yard' was the proper term for the place where Canadians cooled off in the summer; 'garden' was an affected, English term. In Annie's case, the half-acre of lawn surrounding her family home on Prince Edward Island was still called 'the yard', and she found the term 'garden' Upper Canadian, and effete.

'Don't their friends know?' she asked.

'No. Bloody mystery. Probably nothing to it, but the guy who didn't speak to Salter is my chief suspect at the moment.'

'Why?'

'No reason. I just don't like the bugger.'

'Maybe there was a woman?'

'Nobody has said anything about it if there was.'

'Politics, then. What about you and Albert Prine?'

'What about it? I caught him listening to my phone calls.' Salter was immediately irritated. What did this have to do with anything?'

'But you couldn't prove it.'

'No, but the bugger *knows* I caught him. If I had accused him they would have called me paranoid.'

'He *was* listening, though. And you've never told anyone.'

'If I did, he'd soon hear about it and I would have to prove it, or get clobbered.'

'So you haven't talked to him for a year. You don't even mention his name around here any more.'

'No, because sometimes I think you think I imagined it.'

'Oh, I believe you, Charlie. You see what I mean, though.'

'All right.' Salter swallowed his irritation. 'So you're saying these two sort of had something on each other. I don't think it could be politics, though.'

'Money?'

'I don't see how.'

'Sex, then?'

'One of Summers's pals suggested they probably met one night in a body-rub parlour. From what I saw of Dunkley, something like that would bother him, all right. But Summers, I gather, would have been one to make a joke of it, once he got over his embarrassment. He wasn't shy about suggesting they all go to a girlie show in Montreal, but Dunkley was.'

'You mean all these middle-aged professors get away from their wives and they act . . .'

'Just like everyone else. Especially at that age.'

She accepted the tease. 'Charlie, would you go to a show like that, if you were on holiday away from me?'

'No, dear. Only on business.'

But she was concerned now. 'From what you've told me, half these people are having affairs their wives don't know about.'

'Just one, dear: Pollock. And I don't know if he's married.'

'Of course he is.'

Now they were off on a familiar misery, entitled, 'Why Do Married Men Play Around?' with the inevitable sub-theme, 'Do You?' Fortunately Salter was saved by the arrival of Angus around the corner of the house carrying a cricket bat. One of the traditions of Annie's family was that the men went to Upper Canada College, and she had used her trust fund, set up by her grandmother, to keep the tradition going for Seth and Angus. It would have been piggish to object, but their fancy ways made him uncomfortable, and he kept a firm, ironic distance from the goings-on of the quality his sons mixed with, and occasionally brought home.

'Did you win?' he asked now. 'How many bounders did you hit?'

'Boundaries, Dad. None. I was stumped first ball.'

'That sounds bad, son.'

'It is. It means I was out before I even hit one.'

Salter tutted. 'Did you pitch today?' he asked wide-eyed.

'Bowl,' Angus said. 'Bowl, bowl, bowl, bowl. NO!'

'That's enough,' said Annie. 'I'll get you some supper,'

another word she preserved in the face of Upper Canada's 'dinner'.

'Angus won't want any supper,' Salter said. 'He'll have had tea. In the pavilion. Won't you, son?'

The other two ignored him, and his wife moved into the house while his son took her chair, indicating a desire for a chat with his father. This was rare enough for Salter to stop his fooling and take an interest. Angus came to the point immediately.

'Dad, the Civics teacher wants parents to come and give us a talk on what they do. I said I'd ask you.'

Salter was thrown into confusion. While the subject of his career did not crop up much around the house, he had the impression that the boys, once over their 'cops and robbers' phase, were slightly ashamed of him, especially among their moneyed friends. Now here was Angus suggesting he display himself in public. His first instinct was an immediate and derisive refusal, but he was slightly touched, so he played for time.

'Who have you had so far, son?' he asked.

'Pillsbury's father, who's a stockbroker, a chartered accountant, two lawyers, and a big deal surgeon who transplants hearts or something.'

Salter returned to his first instinct. 'No, thanks, son. Too glamorous for me. I'll tell you what. I'll get my sergeant to come over. He used to go round the schools in Safety Week, teaching them to "Stop, Look, and Listen". The kids loved it.'

Angus got up. 'I know. I heard him. I'll tell Mr Secord "no", then.'

'That's right. Tell him all my work is highly confidential.'

Annie returned from getting Angus his supper. '*I* suggested that,' she said. 'He asked me and I said I thought you might. Why don't you?'

'Because I'd feel a horse's arse, that's why,' Salter said

noisily, and picked up his notebook to cut off the discussion. 'Now tell me, where have I heard of Pollock?'

'I don't know. Perhaps, like everyone else, you've heard of him as a famous artist.' Annie was hostile, po-faced.

Never mind. She'd get over it. 'Right, thanks. What does uxorious mean? U, X . . .'

'I know the word. It means dotingly fond of one's wife. Why?'

'Guy called himself that today. Now tell me this . . .'

But Annie had left.

Late that night, in bed, she asked him, 'Charlie, have you had any other women lately?'

He grabbed her in a mock-brutal gesture. 'I haven't had *any* women lately.'

She took his hand away. 'I'm not surprised if that's how you go about it.' She sat up and took off her nightdress. 'Try a little tenderness,' she said.

Afterwards she asked, 'Well, have you?'

'What?' he asked. 'What? Oh, for Christ's sake, go to sleep.'

On Wednesday morning Salter phoned Montreal. He found O'Brien in the office. 'Hello, Onree. Charlie Salter here. I've done the rounds and it looks to me as if the guy we're looking for is in Montreal. Apparently Summers was celebrating something and throwing his money about. He was drunk, too, even before he got into the whisky. I think someone followed him back to the hotel and clobbered him for his money. Then they panicked.'

'You have interviewed all the people he was with?'

'Yes. An unlikely lot. One possibility, but my guess is still a whore and a pimp.'

'Did he spend the night, what do you call it, pub-crawling?'

'More or less. But they only went to three places. Here they are: Maison Victor Hugo, The Iron Horse, and Les

Jardins du Paradis. How's my accent?'

'Bad, Charlie, but I know these places. OK. I'll put a couple of men on it. You think any of them is the most likely?'

'Les Jardins du Paradis. They were in there between nine and ten, and my guess is that the killer was, too.'

'OK. You have seen everybody?'

'No, no. The funeral is this afternoon. I'll go to that. And I want to go down to this squash club where he spent so much time. Then there's the wife, who I'll see tomorrow. Oh yes, I found out who Jane is—you remember the note in his box? She's an old pal of his, apparently, so I don't expect to find anything there.'

'What about those phone numbers on the little sheet of paper in his wallet?'

'Not yet. I'll do that today. But I still think you will be looking for the villain in Montreal.'

'OK, Charlie. This is taking up a lot of your time.'

'Time's what I've got a lot of, Onree. Talk to you later.' Salter hung up and turned to Sergeant Gatenby.

'Frank, would you let "Chiefie" know that this Montreal case is continuing, and I am assuming he wants me to stay with it. And here—' He picked up the IN tray on his desk, piled high with little errands. 'Send these back where they came from and tell them I'm all tied up. And don't take any more.'

'At all? They've got quite used to us doing their extra jobs.'

'Well, they'll have to get unused to it. They can figure out how to dispose of the surplus horse-shit from Central Stables all by themselves. I'm busy.'

'Being busy is being happy,' Gatenby said. He was fond of this kind of 'old country' patter. This time he was right.

The funeral was conducted from a parlour on Yonge Street, between an English Fishe and Chippe Shoppe and a tavern. When Salter arrived there were a dozen people sitting silently facing the closed coffin. He identified the widow and daughter, pale without weeping, dressed quietly but not in black. Pollock was there with Marika Tils; all the people Salter had interviewed plus several others, presumably from the English Department, sat in a group. One other man sat alone, several rows behind this group, and a girl of about twenty sat in the back row. The funeral was private, so only the most determined had come. The service was Anglican, without a eulogy, and was soon done. When the small crowd straggled out, Salter caught the stranger on the sidewalk and introduced himself. 'You were a friend of Professor Summers, sir?' he asked. The man was making no effort to speak to the widow, unlike the others.

'Not really. I used to play squash with him, that's all. Have to find another partner, now.' A summer-weight business suit and a dark tie; hair slightly shorter than the fashion; a completely typical and nearly faceless Bay Street type, although the shirt was cheap and the shoes too old. Now he acted as if he just wanted to get away, as if the funeral had been a duty of the worst kind.

Salter asked him, 'Who am I talking to, sir?'

The other man stopped walking away from him backwards, and contented himself with continually looking around him as if waiting for a car to pick him up. 'Bailey,' he said. 'Arthur Bailey. I'm called Bill, because of the song.'

'And you were his squash partner?'

'That's right. He played some other people, though. Me, mostly, I guess.'

Bailey was in an agony to be gone, and out of the corner of his eye, Salter noticed the young girl in the back row, saying goodbye to Pollock and Marika Tils. He said, 'This is a difficult time, Mr Bailey. Perhaps I could come and find you tomorrow.'

'I don't know anything about him, Inspector. I don't even know what his wife looks like. I just played squash with him.'

'In a situation like this, it helps to know as much as possible about the victim. Perhaps you can tell me why he was suddenly addicted to squash, Mr Bailey. Where can I find you?'

The man looked wretched. 'At the squash club, at four, before my game?' he suggested. 'I may be late. I have to go to our plant at Oakville tomorrow.'

The girl seemed to be saying goodbye. 'Perfect,' Salter said. 'I wanted to get a look at the club. Where shall I wait for you?'

'In the lounge.' Bailey was now moving backwards again.

'Thank you, sir. I'll be there.' Salter turned and swooped down on the girl just as she was starting away. 'Excuse me, miss, could I have a word?'

Professor Pollock crossed the sidewalk and introduced them. 'Molly Tripp, one of Summers's students, Inspector Salter.'

Thank you very much, Salter thought. Now bugger off.

Pollock did a bit of pipe-puffing before he realized that Salter was waiting for him to go. Eventually he made the best of it by inviting the girl to drop by for coffee at any time, and left them alone.

She had shed some tears, but was in control of herself. 'What do you want me for, Inspector?'

'I'm trying to find out all about Professor Summers, miss. You are the first student I've been able to find. What about some coffee?'

'I need something.' She looked at the tavern. 'I'd sooner have a beer.'

Salter led the way in.

'You must have felt pretty strongly about Professor Summers,' Salter began when the beer came.

The girl unbuttoned her raincoat and pulled her arms free. Underneath she was wearing a grey sweater and a dark skirt. Her hair was curly and seemed uncombed. 'I will miss him,' she said. 'He showed me things, and he liked me.'

'A great teacher?'

'No. Some of the students didn't like him. I did, though, and some others.'

'Why?'

'I liked the way he got excited over poetry, especially Romantic poetry. It was from him I realized that poetry is written in a different language, not just prose with rhymes. A lot of people already knew that, I guess, but I didn't.'

Romantic poetry? 'You mean love poems?' he asked innocently.

'No, no. The Romantic period. Wordsworth and Keats, mainly, for him.'

'Why didn't the others like him?'

'They said they didn't get proper notes. They wanted more history. He wasn't very formal in class. And some of the stuff he was talking about he hadn't figured out himself. But he *told* us he hadn't,' she ended, more to herself, apparently echoing an old argument.

'I want to know what kind of person he was. Did you know him—yourself?'

'Personally?'

'Yes.'

'A little bit. I used to go up to his office once in a while and talk to him. As I said, he liked me and we had a nice time talking about stuff.'

'He took an interest in you?'

'He thought I might be able to write a real essay, as he called it. I tried. He told me a couple of weeks ago that the first page of my last essay was the best first page he had had all year. Still only got a B+ though!'

While she was talking, Salter ordered two more beers. He could see why Summers liked Molly Tripp. He had very little to ask her himself, but a very great desire to sit with her for a while longer and watch her talk. She was nice.

'What made the essay so good? The first page, I mean.'

'I read it this afternoon. It sounded like him talking, you know?' She smiled as if she and Salter were talking about a mutual friend.

'And that was it? You were a good student?'

'Yeah, I guess so. Oh, shit, I see what you're getting at. He didn't try to get my pants off. He wasn't a groper.'

That is what I wanted to know, thought Salter, but I may have screwed this up. He acted puzzled. 'Huh?' he said.

'We talked about poetry, is all. We talked some personal stuff sometimes, but not very much.'

Salter thought of a way to cover his interest, to make it official.

'Professor Summers was not in the habit of seducing his students, then?' There. How did that sound? Nice and pompous?

'Hell, no. Oh, there was something there when I was in his office, Inspector. Isn't there always between any man and woman?'

Salter tested this against several ladies he knew, and thought, No. He nodded in agreement.

'The other kids said he spent half the time in class with his eye on me, but I think I was his litmus test. He watched me to see if what he was saying was making sense. I did like him, too. I kissed him once.'

'When?'

'The last time I saw him. Last week. He'd just told me he'd given me an A for the course because of a good exam. He was as pleased as I was, so I gave him a big smacker when he wasn't watching.'

'What did he do?'

'He just sat there looking pleased. Now I want to go.'
She stood up. The tears were streaming down her face.

'Where can I find you?' Salter asked. 'Just in case.'

'Here.' She gave him a card. 'I started work on Monday
as the assistant to the assistant creative director at an
advertising agency, and I have cards already.' She belted
up her raincoat. 'I hope you find this character,
Inspector. What's your real name?'

'Salter,' he said startled. 'Charlie Salter is my real
name.'

'Well, lotsa luck, Charlie.'

They left the tavern and Salter watched her walk away.
Her stride was long and she walked slightly hunched up as
if a gale was blowing. At the corner she turned and saw
him still there, and waved. Salter waved back and
pretended to be looking for his car keys. He would have to
see her again, he decided.

That night, after supper, Annie said, 'I've invited your
father to eat on Sunday.'

Seth groaned theatrically. 'I'll miss Walt Disney. He
doesn't like the TV on.'

Angus said, 'I have to do my essay in the main library
on Sunday. I'll just have a hamburger at Mac's.'

There was a silence while they waited for Salter to start
shouting.

Annie said quickly, 'You can watch Walt Disney
upstairs. And you can come home by six, Angus. Your
grandfather only comes once a month.'

Angus said, 'But this essay is important, Mum. Besides,
I don't like lamb.'

'Nor do I,' Seth said. 'I hate lamb and stuff.'

Annie said, 'It doesn't have to be lamb.'

Salter said, holding on to his temper, 'You can have a
choice, lamb or beef.'

Angus said, 'Couldn't we have poached salmon with that terrific white stuff on it?'

'You know bloody well your grandfather doesn't eat salmon.'

'Lasagna, then.'

'Or any Italian food. Or French, or Greek, or Chinese food. Now knock it off you two. We'll have roast beef, and you'll like it, and you can watch the upstairs TV turned down low. After you've said hullo to him.'

'Walt Disney's no good in black and white.'

'Fine. Don't watch him, then. Now shut up, the pair of you.'

This was the true clash of cultures in the Salter home. Unlike the thoughtful, ever-accommodating relatives of his wife, his own father was a narrow-spirited misanthrope who was getting steadily worse in his old age. He watched television, calling most of it 'bloody American twaddle', and visited the tavern at the end of his street to moan with one or two cronies. He was a former maintenance man with the Toronto Transit Commission who had retired to a tiny flat in the East End of the city near the street-car barn. They saw very little of him, because he was an ordeal. Salter telephoned him once a week, and visited him whenever he was in the area. Annie, however, insisted on their duty to him and he ate his Sunday dinner with them once a month. She had tried him with every delicacy in her repertoire, and he ate them all with the same comment, 'Very nice, I suppose, but I like a proper dinner on Sundays. So did Charlie, once.' A proper dinner was one with gravy and custard. In spite of all attempts by Annie to make him smile, his visits were joyless. The real difficulty lay in coping lightly with his prejudices in front of the children. He was anti-semitic from his youth, and he had since developed a prejudice against every class and race but his own, the poor Anglo-Saxons. No visit was complete without some reference on his part to 'them Jews', the 'Eyeties', or the 'Nig-nogs' who were responsible for his depressed social and financial condition. He watched Annie for any sign that she was patronizing him, and criticized the behaviour of the boys continually until he provoked a flare-up of reaction in Annie or Salter. After a small row, he shut up, satisfied, with a remark like, 'Sorry I spoke. I was just trying to be helpful.' Once he caught Angus in a kilt (another family tradition that Annie had brought to Toronto); this offended the old man in several ways at once, including his anti-Scottish prejudice, and he wondered loudly to Salter, if the boy wasn't turning into 'a bit of a pansy.'

Now Salter cut the conversation off and brought out his notebook. 'I've got some phone calls to make,' he said. 'Stay off the phone for half an hour, will you.'

The boys disappeared, still grumbling, and Salter sat down by the phone. He looked first at a list of numbers that he had transcribed from the scrap of paper in Summers's wallet. 'Do these numbers mean anything to you?' he asked his wife. 'A couple look like phone numbers, but the others don't.' He handed her the list.

She studied it for a while. 'Hold on,' she said. I thought so. This one is his Eaton's Account; this one is the number he used to get money from one of those banking machines. Those two are phone numbers. That one I don't know. It looks like the combination for a lock.'

'Well done. Now all I have to do is phone these two and I'll know all about his private life.'

'Any ideas yet?'

'The same one I started with. It looks like he was done in by accident, by a prostitute or her pimp. In the meantime, I've got interested in the guy, and I'm trying to find out what kind of person he was, just in case we have one of those clever murders, complete with motive and everything. So far, I've found out he wasn't a bad teacher, and some people liked him and some didn't. He had one real enemy and two good friends in the department.'

'Both men?'

'A man and a woman. And there is a student who liked him. And a woman he used to have a drink with, once a year, out of town. That's it.'

'Did the woman in the department like him a lot?'

Salter gritted his teeth. Annie's remark grew from the problem that always lay between them. She was everything a man could want in a wife except for a continual low-burning jealousy, which had grown partly out of the swinging times they lived in. As she understood the scene, no one was faithful these days, and she was constantly alert to the possibility that her husband, whom she saw as an ideal prize, would be picked off by some other woman. As Salter put it once to a woman whose friendship he had retained in the teeth of Annie's hostility, 'Her friends tell her how lucky she is that I don't screw everyone in sight, and she takes that to mean that they are all ready to lie down whenever I say the word. They are all divorced and it makes her nervous.' In fact, Salter had been unfaithful (with the same woman friend) only once, and he was such a poor liar that Annie had suspected immediately. After that he found fidelity the comfortable way to live. He loved his wife, and wished she would relax. When he tried to tell her this, she said only, 'If I relax, you might.' And that, as his woman friend pointed out, was probably true.

Now Annie asked, 'They weren't lovers, then?'

'She says not,' Salter replied.

'You asked her?'

'I'm a copper,' he shouted. 'I'm trying to find out who killed someone. You start by trying to find out who might have wanted to.'

'Is she attractive?'

Oh, fuck it. 'The interesting thing,' he said, 'Is that I

like everyone who liked him, man, woman and child. But
I didn't much take to the ones who didn't. That doesn't
mean that this woman gave me a hard-on, or that
Summers was banging her after hours in the library. It
just means that I might have liked Summers, too.'

'All right, Charlie, make your phone calls.'

The first phone call was embarrassing. The number
turned out to be that of Summers's squash-playing friend,
Bailey, whom Salter had seen at the funeral. 'Sorry, Mr
Bailey. I just wanted to check our appointment. Four
o'clock tomorrow, at the club? Thanks. See you then.'
There was no reply to the second number. Salter
consulted his notebook and dialled again. 'Miss Homer?
Miss Jane Homer? Inspector Salter here. Metro Police. I'd
like to talk to you about Professor Summers. I believe you
were in contact with him in Montreal.'

The voice was thick and strained. 'Yes. I never saw
him, though. What do you want?'

'To talk to you, please. Mainly about Summers's
background. May I come to your office in the morning?'

'All right. I get there about ten o'clock. I am the Dean
of Women at Wollstonecraft Hall. On Harbord Street.'

'I'll find it. At ten o'clock, then. Fine.'

Salter consulted another piece of paper, Summers's
hotel bill with the record of two calls Summers had made
on Friday afternoon. Again, there was no reply to the
first. The second one produced a recorded message to the
effect that the offices were now closed and he should call
again tomorrow. That was that, then. Salter put his
notebook away, and went upstairs to his wife's sewing-
room, where she kept all her old college books. He found
what he was looking for, Volume II of *Representative
Poetry*, and thumbed through it looking for Wordsworth
and Keats. The first Wordsworth poem he found was
about fifty pages long, and he kept looking until he
found one that had fewer than a hundred words. Slowly,

stumblingly, he learned the first two lines, a total of fourteen words. When he was sure of them, he turned to Keats. Again he had trouble finding one to his purpose, so he chose, arbitrarily, the last poem and picked out two lines in the final verse that sounded 'poetic'. Once more he set himself to learn them. More difficult, these, because he was not sure what the lines meant. He sat there, mumbling, as his wife appeared. 'What's going on, Charlie?' she asked, staring at the book.

'It's Summers,' he said in some confusion. 'He specialized in Romantic poetry. I was just trying to see what that was all about. Not very lively, is it?' He smiled falsely.

'Who have you been talking to today?'

'Oh, for Christ's sake,' he shouted. 'I'm just getting into the man's mind. That's all.'

She looked surprised at his reaction, but did not press him further, merely picked up a piece of material she had come for and went back downstairs.

Salter waited until she was well out of hearing and went back to his homework. He had Wordsworth cold, but had to mumble away at the Keats for another five minutes before he felt sure of it.

CHAPTER 4

At the office the next morning, Gatenby greeted him with a message from the Superintendent. 'He wants to hear from you about how this Montreal case is going,' he said.

'I've got an appointment at ten. Is he free now?'

'He said he would be in all morning. He was very keen to hear from you.'

'All right. I'll do it now. I'm going to be out the rest of the day.'

'Quick cup of coffee first? Won't take a minute.'

'All right.'

'Little bit of sugar, just to take the edge off?'

Salter had recently been making a stab at dieting. Gatenby showed his interest by tempting him continually, like an old granny with a pocketful of sweets that the children are forbidden to eat.

'No, Frank,' Salter said, hardly irritated at all. 'Annie said I mustn't.'

Superintendent Orliff was not a friend of Salter's, but neither was he an enemy. The Superintendent had no enemies, a state he had achieved by keeping his distance from anyone who made a lot of waves. He was a small, neat man whose desk was stacked with a dozen tidy piles of paper, each one representing some aspect of his work. He kept records of everything, including all verbal transactions, and the piles grew until the particular project was, or seemed to be (for Orliff was a careful man), finished, when it was put with other piles on the shelves lining his office. Eventually the piles were put into cabinets, but not until they had been dead for a long time. Orliff saw himself as a civil servant surrounded by politicians, and while his opinion was regularly sought, he rarely gave it, offering instead only information. He did not bury himself in his work (one of the piles on his desk contained material about his retirement plans; another charted the progress of a cottage he was building), but he recorded it thoroughly. While the various factions in the organization grouped and regrouped themselves, he sat back, available and promotable. His superiors could trust him to be loyal: his subordinates knew he had no favourites. When the former Superintendent had been promoted, he had taken over the job without opposition. He sat in his office now, waiting for Salter to deliver his report.

Salter said, 'As of now it looks like a mugging. I still have a couple of people to question, but those I've seen so far don't look very likely.'

Orliff put his finger on the transcript from Montreal. 'No robbery,' he said.

'No robbery,' Salter agreed. 'But they probably panicked. Hookers who try this trick are not killers. Maybe she had a new boy-friend who was showing off.'

'They agree in Montreal?'

'I speak to Sergeant O'Brien every day. He'd rather have me find a killer with a nice motive here, but, yes, he's looking for a likely pair.'

'So. A middle-aged English Professor goes to a convention, has a little fling and he's unlucky.'

'Yes, sir. That's funny, because he told everyone that it was his lucky day.'

'What did he mean?'

'I haven't found out yet.'

'Uh. So someone sees a party of profs, a bit pissed, our man throwing his money about, at a tit-show, you say?' Orliff smiled companionably at Salter. 'As one middle-aged man to another, being middle-aged, the young girls get him going, so he dumps his friends and finds himself a hooker. Not so hard because she has already got him picked out and is waiting for the nod, maybe already arranged while his friends weren't looking. Back at the hotel he gets undressed, they have a drink, the boy-friend arrives. Our man objects—maybe threatens to call the police—you never know—and all hands panic. Boy-friend clobbers him, then the real panic. That it?'

'I expect so, sir. Something like that.'

'What's the problem with it?' There was no aggression in the Superintendent's voice. If there was a problem he didn't want Salter to make a fool of himself.

'I'm not happy with it yet. There's something screwy. He'd drunk too much. As one middle-aged man to another, sir, he wanted his bed.'

'He was a professor. Maybe they can keep going longer.' Orliff smiled to show he was joking.

'Nobody at the hotel saw a whore, sir.'

'Like I say, he was a professor. Cunning. He would have slipped her past them, all right.'

'Even drunk?'

'Sure.'

'It's possible, sir, but it's got no life in it. It lacks verisimilitude.'

'Say that again.'

'Verisimilitude, sir. It means believability.'

'Does it, by Christ. You mean it may be true, but it won't play?'

'Well, yes, but in this case I think that means it may not be true.'

'It sounds likely to me,' Orliff said agreeably.

'It's probably true, but . . .'

'Now what?'

'I'm just trying to put myself in this man's shoes. Here I am in Montreal, feeling good because I've just had a stroke of luck—any kind, but it probably involves money because I'm taking the boys out for dinner, a hundred and thirty dollars' worth. (My guess is that professors are a tight lot.) So, I've drunk a fair amount and I feel good, all the time I'm thinking about my luck, whatever it is. Would I feel like a whore? Right then and there? I don't think so. I think Summers just went home in a cab.'

'I see—psychology. After a big win at the track you feel like celebrating, not screwing.'

'More or less, sir, yes.'

'I don't know, Salter. I've never won a lot of money. Tit-shows make *me* horny, don't they you? They are supposed to.'

'Well, yes, sir, and I expect they made the others feel that way, which is why they are all suggesting that

Summers must have picked up a whore. But . . .'

'All right, all right. So what's your theory?'

'If there was a whore, sir, I think it would happen later, after he'd climbed down a bit from his high. He would have had to use the bell-boy—he wouldn't know any call-girls in Montreal, or anywhere else. And O'Brien says the hotel staff swear they saw and heard nothing like that.'

'The bell-boy is lying,' Orliff offered.

Salter felt all the weight of a weary and unintelligible world fall on him. He gave in.

'All right, sir. I'll pack it in. I'll phone O'Brien and tell him that's it.'

'No, no. I'm just doing my job. Giving you a hard time. What's the rest of your alternative theory?'

'There's a piece missing somewhere, probably connected with his lucky day. Whoever killed him did it for more money than was in his wallet, or for envy or revenge. He could have told someone what his lucky day was all about.'

'This guy Dunkley. We've got him on file, you say?'

'He was arrested once for disturbing the peace outside the American Embassy. He's in most of the protests.'

'One of them, is he?' Orliff was mildly interested. It was his strength that he did not feel any enmity towards the citizens who tried to make life difficult for him, the robbers, the rapists, and the civil disobedience crowd. 'Without them,' he would say, 'we wouldn't have a job, some of us.' He fingered the report for a few moments. 'You want to stay on this?' he asked. 'We aren't too busy at the moment.'

And you can always spare me, anyway, thought Salter. 'Yes,' he said. 'Until I find out more about Summers and his luck.'

'Many more possibilities?'

'I haven't talked to the wife yet. Then there's this Jane Homer woman. And I have to talk to his pals at the squash club. At least I want a better idea of the man who got killed, and the kind of man who might have killed him.'

'All right. Don't spring any surprises on me, though. Keep me in touch.' Salter got to the door before Orliff spoke again. 'By the way, this isn't the dregs. I talked to the Deputy in Montreal. He said O'Brien speaks highly of you. I told our Deputy. He was pleased because we owe Montreal a favour. It wouldn't do you any harm if this squared the books.'

Salter understood. Just possibly, if he got lucky, he might find himself moving across the desert again, on the way to the fertile land on the other side.

He still had some time before he had to meet Jane Homer, so he paid a rare visit to the canteen for a cup of coffee. The only other occupant was an inspector in the homicide division whom Salter had known slightly in the old days. They nodded to each other, and Salter sat down at the same table.

'What are you up to these days, Charlie?' the detective asked, pleasantly enough. His name was Harry Wycke, and Salter had no real reason to suppose him hostile. They had never crossed each other, and by now most of his old enemies, like his old cronies, rarely bothered him, but he assumed they were all still relishing his demise. Annie said he was paranoiac, to which Salter replied that even the constable in charge of records gave his requests for information a very low priority when he was busy.

'I'm investigating a murder—in Montreal,' Salter said.

'How does that work, then?'

'A Toronto professor got himself killed in Montreal. I'm helping out at this end.' Was this a problem? Was he poaching on homicide's territory?

'Tough shit. What are you doing, exactly?'

'I think I'm supposed to be looking for a motive. Just in

case there's someone here who might have done it.'

'Wife? Lover?'

'Not the wife. And no lover so far. Someone clobbered him in a hotel room.'

'Whore, maybe?'

'Or a pimp. It looks possible, but they left behind a wallet full of money.'

'They got scared. Did he have any enemies?'

'That's what I'm supposed to find out. So far, I haven't found anyone who looks like a killer.'

'What do killers look like, Charlie? The ones I know all look different. Couldn't be a professional, could it?'

'The mob, you mean. Christ, I don't think so. He was a *professor*. Besides, don't they warn you first, like breaking your legs?'

'They've given that up now. Too much publicity. Now they just leave a little bomb. Then it could be anybody, unless you are on the inside and know who sent it.'

'This guy *was* a gambler, Harry. You think that a bookie would do that?'

Wycke laughed. 'No, I was just kidding. Well, I wish you luck, Charlie. Most killers are easy—you find them two blocks away covered in blood. The thoughtful ones can be very, very hard. How come they gave it to you?'

'I think you boys were too busy. And I'm just helping out,' Salter said cheerfully.

'That's right, we are. We probably looked at it and gave it back. Still, if you need any help, let me know.'

'Thanks.' Salter dipped his toe into the waters of fraternal feeling. 'This stuff is pretty new to me. I might be glad to give you a shout if I get in too deep.'

'Any time. You know where my office is.' Wycke finished his coffee and stood up. 'I won't trip you up,' he said.

Salter understood, and felt a twinge of grateful

warmth. He had been lonely for some time. 'Thanks,' he said. 'Thanks.'

Wollstonecraft Hall, a red sandstone building on Harbord Street, was built by a dissenting church to protect young ladies from the city when they were not in class, but in the 'sixties it had been forced to swing with the times and had become a mixed residence. As he walked through the halls, Salter passed young men and women in about equal numbers, chatting in groups and pairs, and, in one case, embracing feverishly as if war had been declared.

The Office of the Dean of Women was open, and Salter pushed the door back and walked in. A secretary looked up from her typewriter, and he introduced himself. She was the drabbest girl he had seen for some time; she looked as though she had been hired for her plainness by the original sex-fearing governors of the residence. Her glasses, steel-rimmed, round and tiny, were balanced on the end of her nose; her thick blonde hair was cut in a straight line, parallel with the bottoms of her ears; she wore a brown smock that looked like a shroud. Salter was appalled and piteous. 'Is Miss Homer in?' he asked. 'She's expecting me.'

The girl stood up, took her glasses off, and smiled, transforming herself like the heroine of a musical comedy. She had beautiful teeth, and the shroud, when she was upright, clothed a perfect figure. It's a style, thought Salter. They do it deliberately.

The girl went into the inner office and reappeared with another wonderful smile. 'Miss Homer says you can go right in,' she said. She put her glasses on and went back to posing as a hag in front of her typewriter.

Miss Homer was another surprise. She was about thirty-five, light gold hair, a buff-coloured denim suit, brown-and-white striped shirt, gold bangles on each wrist, gold

rings in her ears, and shoes made of tapestry. At first
Salter thought she was sun-tanned, but as he approached
to shake hands he realized she was so thickly freckled that
the freckles seemed alive and she seemed to be blinking to
keep them out of her eyes. Salter, who had been
expecting a grey-haired matron in golf shoes, found
himself shuffling his feet.

'Would you like some coffee?' she asked.

'Thanks. Yes, please.' He sat down in the armchair she
indicated, one of a pair arranged by a low table. To his
further surprise, instead of calling her secretary, she went
to a table by the wall and poured two cups from a
percolator. Ah yes, he thought. Secretaries do not make
coffee these days, especially on the frontier of the
movement.

The room was a relief after the utilitarianism of Douglas
College. On one wall a huge block of photographs of
various kinds formed a mural. On another hung a large
framed thing made of bits of cloth. The desk was a sheet
of heavy glass on two trestles. All this Salter had time to
take in before she returned with the coffee.

She hunched over her cup and waited for him to begin.

Salter showed her the note which she barely glanced at.

'Yes, that's my note. I'd forgotten about it. Is that why
you are here? I never saw Professor Summers.'

'Were you a good friend of his?'

'Once. Not any more. David was an old colleague. I
taught at Douglas while I was doing my thesis.'

'How long ago?'

'Six years. I graduated five years ago, and got this job.'

'Did you often see him in Toronto?'

'No, never. Except by accident, of course.'

'But you arranged to meet him at the conference?'

'At conferences like that you pick up with people you
don't otherwise see. I often had a drink with the Douglas
College people.'

'Were you and Professor Summers in the same field?' Salter asked out of his new knowledge.

'What? Oh no. My field is women's journals.'

'Like *Chatelaine*?' Salter asked, surprised at what English Literature covered.

'No, no. Diaries. I got interested first in Dorothy Wordsworth, and went on from there. As a matter of fact, David was interested in my thesis topic, which concerned journals as literary forms. I think he started one of his own because of me, but I never saw it.'

'Let me see, then. You arrived at the conference and left a note in his box. Wasn't he in his room? What time did you leave the note?'

'About six. No, there was no answer from his room.'

'And that's all the contact you had with him?'

'Yes.' She got up to refill her cup.

'How long did you stay in Montreal?'

'I left on Saturday afternoon, with the people from Douglas. Everyone heard at lunch-time what had happened and I was too upset to stay. Besides, people were talking about it, people who didn't know him, as if it was an exciting thing, like a president being assassinated.' As she replaced her cup on the coffee table it rattled in its saucer.

'I see. That's that, then. You have nothing more to tell me?'

She shook her head and then began to shiver, trembling at first, then violently. When her teeth began to chatter, Salter shouted for the secretary, who ran in and held her until the shivering subsided.

'I'm sorry,' the Dean said, when she had recovered enough. 'I seem to be a bit of a mess.'

'Delayed shock, I should imagine,' Salter said. 'I should go to bed and call your doctor. If I want you again, I'll let your secretary know.'

In the outer office Salter asked the secretary. 'Has that happened before?'

'Yes. A lot. She's hardly stopped since she came back from Montreal. I thought she was all right today, but you set her off again.'

'I didn't realize she was so fragile, miss.'

'She's not. I don't know why this is so hard on her.'

Salter left. Dean of Women overreacts to routine questioning, he thought. I wonder why?

It was a long time since Salter had gone home for lunch. From the early days of their marriage he associated it with 'nooners', making love in the daytime, preferably on the floor. Did the young officers still do that? He and Annie had not done it for years, but now as she stood at the sink he put his arms round her waist and squeezed her in something more than a friendly hug. She twisted in his arms and looked at him, startled and worried, but game. 'If you want,' she said. 'But I'll have to turn the pot down to simmer.'

'Fuck the pot,' Salter whispered, and hugged her close. 'All right,' she said. He let her go. 'We'll save it,' he said.

'Who have you been questioning today?' she asked suspiciously.

'Just an old bag who looks after the morals of young ladies. You are the one who turns me on.'

Over their soup and sandwiches, he talked. He came finally to the Dean of Women..

'She's hysterical, and she's lying, because she's frightened, I think,' he said. 'But I don't know why. I don't think she's a villain.'

'Then why is she so upset?'

'I'll find out. Whatever it is, it is something to do with Summers.'

Before he left, Annie asked him about the holidays. He felt like being gracious. 'Make whatever arrangements you like,' he said. 'The boys will be happy, and I don't have a better proposal.'

'What's got into you lately, Charlie?'

'I'm busy,' he said, and opened the front door. As he stepped out he almost walked into a small dark-haired woman in an apron who began screaming at him.

'You Mr Salter?' she asked. 'Come quick. Lady I work for gonna be killed. Come quick.'

Annie reappeared from the kitchen. 'It's Rosa. Mrs Canning's cleaning lady. Quick, Charlie. Something must be wrong.'

It was one of the penalties of being a policeman.

Salter and Annie followed the cleaning lady at a trot across three front yards to Mrs Canning's house. There in the kitchen they found her, standing terrified in the corner, clutching her two young children. 'He's upstairs,' she said. 'In the front bedroom.'

Salter climbed the stairs cautiously to the second floor and went along the hall to the front bedroom. The door was closed, and Salter shouted through it without getting a response. Then he threw the door open and stood back. Nothing happened. Salter moved to the doorway and looked around the room. All the curtains had been drawn so that there was only a gloomy orange light to see by, but it did not take much light to see that the room had been wrecked. The bedroom was also used as a study, and the floor was two feet deep in books and all the other bric-à-brac—clocks, mirrors, ashtrays, lamps—that had formerly stood on the tables and shelves. In the big double bed, under the covers, was a young giant, his eyes open, watching Salter.

'What the hell do you think you're doing?'

'You are trespassing,' the boy said. 'This is my room.'

Salter left, closing the door behind him, and called down the stairs to Mrs Canning. 'What's going on?' he asked. 'He says that's his room.'

'It's *my* room. Mine and Albert's. This is *my* house. He just appeared half an hour ago asking if I was running a baby farm. He's got bathing trunks on.' Mrs Canning was nearly demented. 'I had to keep talking until Rosa came back. I've never seen him before.'

Annie said from beside her, 'He must be mad, Charlie. Be careful.'

'Phone Frank,' Salter said. 'Tell him what's happening. Tell him we need a car and two big men. I'll stay here.'

While they were waiting for help, Mrs Canning calmed down a bit and suggested where the intruder might have come from.

'We rent the third floor to a girl at the CBC,' she said. 'He must have been up there and come down when she left this morning.'

'Phone her,' Salter said.

In a minute it was confirmed. He had arrived from Europe the day before and had been given a bed for the night on the third floor. He had seemed very tired, but the girl had not noticed anything strange about him.

Very quickly the squad car arrived, bringing not only two constables but Gatenby himself. 'You don't mind, do you, boss?' he asked like a child pleading to be allowed up late. 'I haven't been outside the office for months.'

The assault party formed up in the hallway on the second floor. Salter explained the situation and the two officers pulled out their guns, causing the women on the stairs to make frightened noises, but they only emptied the shells into their pockets and re-holstered the weapons. One of the constables said something to Salter, and he turned to his wife.

'They won't hurt him,' he said. 'But they might have to hold him tight, or even handcuff him so that *they* don't get hurt. You'd better go back into the kitchen.'

They got ready to move down the hall, and Gatenby stopped them. 'Let me have a go, first,' he said. 'I might be able to talk to him.'

The others looked doubtful, but Gatenby pleaded. 'Is there a dressing-gown in the room, lady?' he called down the stairs.

'On the door,' she said.

'Right you are.' Gatenby turned to the others. 'Come and get me if I holler,' he said with a wink, and walked into the bedroom, closing the door behind him.

There was a murmuring of voices from inside the room. One of the constables asked Salter, 'You sure he's all right, sir? He seems a bit old for this kind of thing.'

'I don't know what the hell he's up to,' snapped Salter, 'We'll give him five minutes, then we'll go in.'

But in another minute Gatenby reappeared with the boy, dressed now in a tiny striped robe. Gatenby had his arm around his shoulers and was talking to him soothingly, like an old granny. 'Here we go, then. We'll just go downstairs, won't we, that's it. Out to the car, and we'll take you where we can get you all fixed up.'

Salter led the way and opened the door of the squad car as Gatenby talked the boy into the seat, closing it gently behind him.

'All yours, lads,' he said. 'Take him down to the Comical College. Don't shout at him.'

The policeman looked at each other and at Salter, who shrugged. 'Take him away, lads,' he said.

Salter and Gatenby drove back in silence for a few blocks, then Salter said, 'All right, Frank. What the fuck did you do in there?'

'I used psychology, chief,' Gatenby said, chuckling happily. 'I could see he was just a kid, so I went over to the bed and said straight away, "Do you love your mum?" He said, "Yes." So I said, "Well, if you love your mum, she loves you, so come on up and we'll go and see if we can find her." '

Salter waited. 'And that's it?' he asked, finally.

'That's all. He got up quiet as a lamb and put on that dressing-gown, and that was that.'

'Jesus Christ,' Salter said, after another long pause. 'Jesus H. Christ.'

The interlude over, Salter went back to brooding about Summers. What was his responsibility to O'Brien? To ask questions, watch the whites of their eyes, and see if anyone was lying. So who was? At a guess, he thought, everyone except Usher. But what about? Begin with Carrier. It was possible that Carrier was being his natural gerbil-like self, but he certainly acted like a man with a secret. But a killer? Unlikely. Marika Tils? Even more unlikely, and yet she had seemed to be evading him at the end.

Dunkley was still the obvious choice. Hard to tell if he was lying, because everything he said sounded like rehearsed dogma. He was a man of principle, or a self-righteous prick, depending on how you reacted to him, but did that make him suspicious? Would he lie, much less kill, on principle?

Which left Jane Homer, the Dean of Women. There was also someone with a story she wasn't telling, but what? Did Summers try to rape her, after all these years? Hardly. If she knew anything that would help him she would surely have said so. They were old friends, she and Summers.

What about Summers? He was drunk, he had seen a girlie show, he was in his dressing-gown, there was lipstick on the glass, and he had had a lucky day. Any famous detective would have solved it in five minutes, but all Salter could come up with was the classic 'whore-and-pimp' solution. In the meantime he could think of a number of things he ought to do before he went back to cleaning up Yonge Street. Like having a look at the scene of the crime. And seeing Molly Tripp again.

Back in the office, Gatenby picked up their messages. 'They've all been calling,' he said as if he were reading a children's story to a four-year-old. 'Chiefie, DeeCee, the copper from froggieland. There's no mail, though.'

Wonderful. Not a single silly assignment, or request, for three days. Was it really passing? The Chief was, in fact, the Superintendent's secretary, asking if a written copy of the report on the Montreal case would be forthcoming; the message from the Deputy was to ask if he needed any help. Deduction. He was on the case the Deputy was interested in. A pity he was getting nowhere, even if he was having fun. He phoned O'Brien.

'I have talked to everyone in the area, Charlie. They remember him in the bars, but that's all. I think I've talked to every known character who was in Les Jardins du Paradis when Summers was there, but I can't smell anything.'

'The hotel staff remember anything?'

'I question them every day, just for practice, and to see if they start remembering. Nothing. Why don't you come down and try it yourself?'

'It's your turf, Onree,' Salter said, but thinking, Why don't I?

'My what?' O'Brien asked.

'Your turf. Your manor,' Salter explained.

'Ah yes. Mon fief.'

'I guess so. Onree, I've had a thought. Maybe I will come down. Not to help you out, but just to get a feel of what happened on Friday night. When are you free?'

'Monday would be good.'

'Perfect. I'll come down on the afternoon train.'

'I'll meet you, Charlie. Look for me.'

At 3.30 Salter left for the squash club.

Salter was aware of the new concern for health which had filled the streets of Toronto with men and women trotting about in shorts, and had created an industry devoted to selling fitness. One of the products of this concern was the huge growth of racquet sports, especially squash. Annie had suggested to him more than once that it was a sport that might answer his own need for exercise. Salter watched his growing belly, and listened to himself puff up the stairs, and toyed with the idea, but his overwhelming concern not to look, sound, or feel a fool under any circumstances had kept him from enquiring further. Now he had an official reason to look inside one of the new clubs and he was looking forward to satisfying his personal curiosity.

The Simcoe Squash Club is on the edge of Toronto's downtown shopping district, which is also Toronto's business district. The location makes it ideal for the man or woman who wants a game on his way to or from work, and it is at its busiest in the early morning, the late afternoon, and at lunch-time. It is housed in a converted warehouse, and Salter found it easily, at a few minutes before four, by following the trickle of men with athletic bags who were converging on the large brick building.

A girl seated at the desk inside the door was checking off members as they arrived, confirming bookings in a ledger and taking money. Salter did not introduce himself officially, saying merely, 'I'm meeting Mr Bailey here. He's a member.'

She nodded, and picked up the phone at the same time. 'If you follow those guys — Hi, Joe, that was a real wingding last night — down the stairs — Just a minute, "Hello, Simcoe Squash Club" — hang on, Mary Lou, I've gotta talk to you — Gerry! How *are* you? — through into the lounge — hang on a second — no, sir, all booked at four-forty — don't go away, Mary Lou — you could get a cup of coffee and — WAIT, Mary Lou — OK? He'll see you when he comes in. OK? — now listen, Mary Lou, you know what happened last night? — '

Salter picked out the bits of this that were his and
followed the crowd into a large area full of tables and
chairs. The crowd disappeared, one by one, through a
door in the far corner, and Salter found himself a seat
and looked around. Half a dozen pairs of members
dressed in shorts and looking more or less exhausted and
sweaty were drinking beer. Most of them were in their
twenties, but one pair was white-haired and ten years
older than Salter. One wall of the lounge was made of
glass and formed the back wall of a pair of courts. A game
was in progress on one of the courts, and Salter tried to
follow it. The players leapt and ran, hitting the ball
alternately, sometimes seven or eight times, before one of
the players missed. Salter couldn't follow the ball and
instead concentrated on the players, marvelling at the
way they ran round each other, never crashing into each
other, rarely touching. As he watched, one of them dived
to retrieve a ball low against the wall and smashed his
racquet in two. It looked like an expensive game. Would
he be able to play it? Salter had been a mediocre though
enthusiastic athlete in his youth, reduced in the last few
years to golf, and not much of that. He had left behind all
team sports, he hated the idea of jogging, and his
attention span for formal calisthenics was about a
minute. In fact, apart from golf, he hardly exercised at
all, which is to say for about nine months of the year. He
felt the need. This game looked as though it might
provide the answer—half an hour of competitive frenzy
leading to renewed fitness or a heart attack.

'Are you a member, sir?'

The young athlete standing beside him in squash gear
was obviously an official of some sort.

Salter decided on a touch of rudeness. 'No,' he said.
'Are you?'

'I'm the club pro, sir. In the afternoons I'm also the
manager. Can I help you?'

'I'm waiting for Mr Bailey.'

'Oh yes. Old Bill. Mind if I sit down?' The pro pulled out a chair. 'You thinking of joining?'

'I'm not thinking of anything right now, Mister . . . ?'

'Larry.'

'Right now, Larry, I'm watching these two, and waiting for Old Bill.'

'Do you play yourself, Mr . . . ?'

'Salter, Charlie Salter.'

'Do you play, Charlie?'

Salter continued to be offended by this boy with dark ringlets cascading down his back, now putting himself on first name terms without permission, but the pro's easy manner, like that of a new wave priest, disconcerted him.

'No. I've never even seen the game until today.'

'Like me to explain it?'

No. Why? 'Yes,' he said.

Larry outlined the objectives of the game, the elementary strategies employed, and then supplied a brief commentary on the game in progress. Salter was intrigued. The pro said, 'Like to have a go?'

'Now?'

'Why not?'

'I'm not dressed for it.'

'I can fix that. We have cupboards full of stuff that's been left behind in the washing machines. All clean. Shoes, too. I'll find you a racquet.'

'No. Some other time maybe.'

'Tomorrow? Come down in the afternoon. I'll give you a lesson. Show you around.'

'Why?'

'If you like it you might become a member. I get a commission on everyone I sign up.'

'No secrets with you, are there, Larry? What does it cost?'

'I won't charge you anything for tomorrow.'

'I know that. I mean this place, a year.'

'Three hundred the first year. Two hundred after that.'

'And the cost of each game?'

'The courts are free except between eleven-thirty and one-thirty, and after four. If you played during the day it wouldn't cost you anything.'

'Who would I play?'

'No problem. Lots of people looking for a game.'

'My age?' Salter asked shyly.

'Our oldest member is seventy-two. We have lots of members in their fifties and sixties.'

'I'm forty-six.'

'No problem. I'll see you tomorrow, then, about three.'

'What? I don't know. Yes. Maybe. All right. I'll let you know if I can't come. By the way—' Salter looked at the clock; he still had five minutes—'did you know Mr Summers well?'

Larry looked pious. 'Yes. He was a good friend of Bill's, of course, that's how you would know him. Terrible thing to happen.'

Salter let this pass. 'Did he play much?' he asked.

'Every day. He and Bill used to get into a battle royal every day. Bill is going to be lost without him.'

'A battle royal?'

'They played hard. Not terrifically good, but they went at it like a couple of one-armed rug-beaters. The loser paid.'

'Paid what?'

'They always played for beer. The loser paid for the beer. Hey, Susie,' he called to a waitress. 'This is Mr Salter, a friend of Dave Summers. I was just telling him about the great games he used to have with Bill Bailey.'

The waitress struck a sad attitude. 'Oh, those guys used to really beat up a storm, you know? And you always knew who was going to pay, like. Real kids they were. I mean, you know, for men, like, mature men, it was funny to see how bad it was for the one who lost. Especially Mr Bailey.' She raised her eyebrows, shook her head, pursed her lips, looked around stagily to see if she were being overheard, all to indicate that Bailey was a poor loser. 'They were at it every night,' she concluded.

'Did they play last week.'

'Oh, sure. They played Thursday night before Mr Summers went to Montreal.'

'Who won?' Salter fixed an expression of warm, sad, piety on his face. He calculated that he had about two more questions before the waitress or the pro asked him why he was asking.

'Oh, gee, I don't know. Wait a minute. Yes, I do. Mr Summers must have won, because he was teasing Mr Bailey, you know, pretending to explain the game to him. Wait a minute, though, he couldn't have won because he paid for the drinks. I think. No. Oh, gee, I don't know. I guess Mr Bailey must have paid, because he was the loser all right.' All this was delivered in the form of a passionate argument with herself.

'I see you're ahead of me, Inspector.' Bailey stood by the table. As the meaning of his words got through to the others, the waitress scuttled, terrified, back to the bar, where she locked herself in conversation with the barman. The pro, however, looked quizically at him. 'Toronto's finest, eh? Here on official business? I guess you don't want a lesson after all. You might have let me know, Inspector.'

'I'd still like a lesson. Do you let coppers join?'

'This is a club for the downtown professional man. That would include you.'

'Then I'll be here tomorrow, at three.'

The pro ducked his curls in a graceful bow, and left, looking like a Restoration beau about to sneak the immortal 'Anyone-for-tennis?' line into the wrong century.

Bailey sat down. 'Thinking of joining the club, Inspector?' he said, too cheerily.

No one is comfortable with the police, Salter thought. 'I don't know. He asked me to give it a try. I might.'

Bailey affected a hearty look. 'If you want some practice, I'll give you a game.'

'I guess you need a new partner. You used to play Summers all the time, you say.'

'We played a lot. We joined together a couple of years ago and we've been kind of seesawing back and forth. Did, I mean. It's hard to start thinking in the past.'

'Did you play him last week?'

'Oh, sure. Every day until he left.'

'Who won on Thursday? The waitress said you had quite a game.'

Bailey thought for a moment. Then, 'He did, I think. Yes, he did. Why?'

'No real reason, Mr Bailey. But it might be useful. For instance, all day Friday, Summers talked about having had a lucky day, and he paid a big dinner bill on Friday night. Now if his wife tells me he was feeling very happy on Thursday night, I'll know it was just squash, nothing to do with whatever was making him so happy on Friday. See.'

Salter felt proud of this pile of rubbish, invented on the spur of the moment to divert Bailey. The reason was that the more he knew about Summers's relationships, the more he would know about Summers, and that included knowing whether he was a good loser or a bad one, and what kind of winner he was, too.

Another man appeared at their table, about fifty, bald as a melon except for a fringe, with the calm, kindly face of a contented accountant. He was clean-shaven, and the fringe of hair had been cut to give him an ecclesiastical air. He looked out of place among all the young stockbrokers and lawyers, but seemed completely at home.

'We were talking about David, Percy,' Bailey said. 'This is Inspector Salter, Percy. Percy Cranmer.'

Cranmer had the hand of a farmer, and he gripped Salter's warmly. 'Very sad,' he said. 'What about his home life? Did he leave any little ones? His wife all right?'

'I think so, Mr Cranmer. He only had one daughter. She's at college.'

'Is that right? We don't know much about each other here, except for squash. I never met Dave's wife.'

Bailey stood up. 'We have a game, Inspector, if that's 'it.'

'That's it, Mr Bailey. Thanks very much. If I want you I'll know where to find you.'

'Like Percy said, Inspector, we don't know much about each other here. I wouldn't have a lot more to tell you about old Dave.'

'I meant about that practice you mentioned. If I join the club.'

'Oh. Right. Sure, Inspector. Any time. Come on Perce.'

Cranmer said, 'Good luck, Inspector. I hope you catch the fella. Poor old Dave.'

Salter did not leave at once. When the two men had been gone for ten minutes he found the staircase connecting the courts, and climbed. There were three levels of court, arranged in blocks of eight, twenty-four in all. On one of the top levels Salter found a gallery overlooking the courts below and he stopped to watch. Bailey and Cranmer were playing in one of the end courts, and by standing back, Salter could watch them without being seen. He was surprised to see that the burly accountant played a delicate game, all flicks and soft shots, while Bailey bashed the ball whenever he got a clear shot. By the frequency of service changes, Salter judged that the two men were about even. They were also, compared to the players Salter had been watching in the lounge, very bad. Bailey constantly mis-hit the ball, and Cranmer was only effective if he could flick it around the front wall. They bumped into each other all the time, often interfering with each other's shots. Bailey was as unsmiling and fierce as the good players downstairs, while Cranmer retained his fatherly smile throughout. Salter came to the conclusion that he should be able to beat either one of them in a week.

It was five o'clock, just the right time to telephone Molly Tripp, the student at the funeral. He was lucky. She was going to an early movie on Bloor Street, but she agreed to meet Salter for a sandwich first, so they arranged to see each other at a café on Cumberland Street.

He arrived before her and ordered a beer. The café was almost deserted for no reason that Salter could see, because he had passed two similar establishments on the street that were jammed with people meeting after work. While he was wondering, Molly arrived.

'Hi,' she said, standing squarely before him, smiling like a child, sure of her welcome. She wore a pair of old blue jeans and a sweat shirt, and she was carrying a yellow slicker.

He stood up. 'Let me get you a sandwich,' he said. He pointed to the menu on the wall which listed a dozen kinds of sandwiches, all unfamiliar to him. 'I'll have a "Reuben, Reuben",' she said. He ordered it, feeling foolish.

'What's a "Reuben, Reuben",' he asked.

'A double Reuben, like a double corned beef on rye.'

'What's a Reuben?'

'Oh, it's great. Corned beef, cheese, and sauerkraut.'

'Uh. You want something to drink? Beer?'

'No. I'll have a sip of yours, though.' She picked up his

mug and took a mouthful. Salter looked nervously around but no one seemed to be watching them.

'There,' she said. 'Great. I love beer but I want to stay awake for the movie. I'd like a coffee, though.'

He placed the order, and they settled down opposite each other.

'You wanted to ask me more stuff about Professor Summers?' she invited. 'I was upset yesterday, but I'm all right now.'

'Yes.' Salter nodded. Her hair which had seemed messy at the funeral now seemed just right. Was it 'carefully tousled' as they used to say? She had a pleasant face which was made more appealing by a slightly affected use of gesture—her eyes went wide with wonder, the corners of her mouth turned down in despair or disappointment, and joy switched on the sun in her face. And she was wearing no brassiere. Salter smiled at her, 'Yes,' he said. 'As I told you yesterday, I am trying to learn as much about Summers as I can. What kind of man he was. Whatever you can tell me about him.'

'So go ahead. Ask.' She smiled encouragingly.

'Was he a good teacher?' Salter asked, again. Who cared? All he wanted was an excuse to keep this girl with him.

'You asked that. I told you. But I've thought about it since then. I still don't know. On the plus side, he knew his stuff, he liked it, and he got excited about it. On the minus side he didn't lay it out in a way that was easy to take down, if you like a lot of notes. So some of the students, especially the girls, got a bit uptight when the exams came around.'

'They didn't all fall in love with him?' Why was he feeling jealous?

She roared with laughter. 'You're a bit out of date, Charlie. Nobody sits swooning in class these days.'

'What do they do these days? Lie down in the

professor's office between classes?'

She sat back in her chair. 'No. Usually we just grab the ones we like by the balls when we meet them in the hall. What kind of question is that?'

Salter felt as if he had just pinched her, spitefully. 'I'm sorry,' he said. 'I don't know what goes on in colleges these days with your generation.'

'What do you *think* goes on?'

'I don't know.' Salter was miserable. 'You hear about swinging professors, you know.'

'Summers didn't swing. I told you, he taught poetry.' She was still sitting back watching him. 'What was it like in your day? Did you go to university?'

'For a while. Listen: "A slumber did my spirit seal; I had no human fears." '

She sat forward, smiling. 'That's Wordsworth. It was one of Summers's favourites.'

'Was it?' Salter clawed his way back into her favour. 'Here's another bit: "While barred clouds bloom the soft-dying day, And touch the stubble plains with rosy hue." That's Keats,' he said.

' "To Autumn",' she said. 'Right. He liked that one, too. 'Are all you guys romantics?'

'No, just me. That was my favourite course,' he lied. 'I dropped out of university after second year.' They were nearly together again, and slightly excited by the exchange.

The 'Reuben, Reuben' arrived and she began to eat while he sipped another beer. Nothing was said until she had made some progress with the sandwich.

Then, 'Good sandwich?' he asked.

'Here,' she said, offering him a bite. He leaned forward to take the corner of the sandwich between his teeth. If anyone is watching this, he thought, they will think we are doing a Tom Jones.

'Nice,' he said, chewing, and taking a sip of beer. 'So.

I've learned about English professors, and I know a little bit more about Professor Summers. Tell me some more.'

She considered. 'He was enthusiastic—have I said that? Sometimes he went pretty far and got worked up about what he was saying.'

'Very emotional?'

'I thought he kind of looked for highs in class.'

'How?'

'He liked the room to turn on to what was happening. If we just sat there, he wasn't much good. He didn't seem to have many notes to fall back on. If he didn't get much response you had the feeling he would just wrap up what he was saying and go on to something else. On a bad day he could do *Paradise Lost* in twenty-five minutes.'

'All twelve books?' Salter asked smugly. In his university course only the first two books were assigned, but it was well known that there were ten more.

'Yes. It didn't always work, though.'

'What about outside the class?'

'What do you mean?'

Salter took a deep breath. Most of all he wanted to avoid sounding like a dirty old man, but one part of him continued to conduct a police investigation. 'Students sometimes know what is going on outside the room,' he said. 'Was there any gossip about Summers?'

'Here we go again.'

But Salter had considered his question. 'All right,' he said. 'I would like to know if you thought he had any close friends or enemies in the college.'

'Or lovers.'

'Or lovers.'

'We wondered about one of his colleagues. This isn't any fun, Charlie.'

'Nor for me. Which one?'

'Marika Tils. They kissed each other hello and goodbye a lot.'

'Everybody does that now. It's called the Elizabethan kiss of greeting,' said Salter, who had read about it in Saturday's paper.

'Yes, well. That's it. She was an Elizabethan friend, then.'

'But no students.'

'I don't think so. He probably had someone like me in every class. But, as I said, it was all poetry.'

'No enemies?'

'Not that I could see.' She finished her sandwich and picked up the check. 'Movie starts in twenty minutes, Charlie. Want to come?'

He took the check from her. 'No, But I'd like to see you again.'

She looked bewildered, and then she laughed. 'Do you think we ought to go on meeting like this?'

Grateful, he said, 'Sometimes new questions crop up and you like to be able to come back.'

'Any time, Charlie,' she said. She looked at the clock. 'My turn?'

'What?'

'My turn. One. Why did you become a policeman?'

Tell her the truth. So he did, just as if he were talking to a stranger in a foreign country, someone he would never see again.

'I was fed up,' he said. 'I'd dropped out of university . . .'

'Why?'

'I found myself counting the number of bricks in the classroom wall while the lecturer was explaining why some poem I hadn't read was so witty. It wasn't his fault. I hadn't tried to read the poem, because it seemed to be in code. To understand the jokes you had to know the Bible. But I was doing the same thing in History, Economics, and Sociology, especially Sociology. I was about to fail the lot, so I quit.'

'Then what?'

'I looked for some action. I tried to get on a ship, but you have to be a member of the Union; if there had been a war on I would have joined the army. I was bored stiff, but everything I thought of trying took five years' training.'

'It sounds a bit adolescent.'

Salter nodded. Strangers were allowed to say things like that. 'Childish,' he agreed. 'I wasn't ready to settle down so I guess I hadn't grown up.'

'So why the police?'

'I met a guy. I played hockey on the weekend pickup team — you know, the only ice time you can get is twelve o'clock on Sunday night — and one of the guys on the team was a detective. I'd just been rejected for a job I didn't want anyway, selling insurance, and he said why didn't I try out for the police? So here I am.'

'Did you like it?'

'I loved it. I was lucky. I did a little bit of everything at first, before I got into administration.'

'That sounds dull.'

'It wasn't. I was full of ideas and I lived and breathed the job. I got sent on study tours to look at other police forces; I got to say what I thought we should change — I had a terrific time. The three stripes came early, and then I got to be an inspector. That was five years ago.'

'Then?'

'Then the man who was looking after me all this time, who I thought would become deputy, didn't, and he retired and I found I had made a lot of enemies, so I was out in the cold.'

'Sounds like General Motors.'

'I guess so. Anyway, I got shifted out of the centre of things and I've been doing errand work ever since.'

'Is it all over?'

'I thought it was. Now, I'm not so sure. I'm enjoying

myself this week.'

'Are you married?'

'Yes, twice.'

'What happened the first time.'

'It lasted a year.'

'Yes, but what happened?'

'We broke up, got divorced.'

'Yes, but why?'

'She became a hippie, one of the first. She didn't like being married to a square, and I wouldn't let her smoke pot. It was a big deal then.'

'But you got lucky the second time.'

'Yes. It's not all hearts and flowers but I'm still married.'

'Is she pretty?'

'Everybody else says so.'

'Do you have a good sex life?'

Salter looked around again. 'I haven't compared lately,' he said. 'But it's a bloody sight better than I was having at your age.'

She laughed. 'Good,' she said. 'Now I have to go.' She put out her hand in a weirdly formal gesture. 'Once more, Charlie, I hope you catch him.'

He still had some beer to finish so he stayed in the café and watched her cross the parking lot and walk between the two buildings on her way to Bloor Street.

After dinner, overwhelmed by a desire to be agreeable, he helped his wife with the dishes, taking the opportunity to kiss her on the neck, an area he was fond of.

'Go away, goat,' she said. 'Or I'll cover you in suds.'

He dropped the dishtowel on her head to blindfold her, undid the button on her slacks and nearly got the zipper down, preparatory to raping her, dramatically, up against the 'fridge. ' "Strange fits of passion I have known," ' he said.

'Not so strange,' she said dodging. 'But you'll have to wait. Dorothy is coming in from next door to show me how to make a new kind of patchwork square.'

Half an hour later she came upstairs to look for the sewing-basket and found him posing in front of the mirror wearing a jockstrap.

He failed to look embarrassed, so she tried a joke. 'If you want to try my underwear on, don't tear it,' she said.

'Me Thor,' he said, in reference to an old love-making joke. 'For your information, madam, I am going to play squash tomorrow.'

'In that?'

'And my old tennis stuff. Do you know where it all is?'

'What's this all about?'

'I'm going to play squash. Get fit again, like you suggested.'

'Why now? What's going on?'

'Oh, for Christ's sake, nothing's going on. I just decided to take up squash, is all.' He told her the story of Bailey and the club, and his curiosity about Summers's passion for the game.

'Well, enjoy yourself. But take it easy.' She looked at the slight belly. 'I don't want to be widowed by a heart attack.'

'You think I'm too old?' he asked.

'Of course not, dear.' She tried to make up by tweaking his jockstrap, letting it snap back against him. 'Have a good game,' she said. 'But leave something for me.'

'Ha, ha, ha. Randy bitch.' Salter turned happily back to the mirror. He felt as if he were on holiday.

CHAPTER 5

He woke smiling from his first good dream in a year. He sat up and grabbed at the memory before it faded. He was in charge of a World Centre. People came to him with their problems. He was the World Centre for All Problems. Telephones rang. 'World Centre here,' he would say. 'Can I help you?' He solved them all. Salter shook Annie awake, 'I'm the World Centre,' he said. 'Can I help you?'

'Orange juice,' she said, pulling her nightdress tight around her knees and turning away.

'Right,' he said, and jumped out of bed to fetch it.

He was not looking forward to interviewing Summers's wife, and he had put if off as long as possible. Now she was the last one, and he had an appointment with her for ten o'clock that morning. Her house was on Stouffville Avenue, in an area known as Deer Park, no more than a mile from his own house, and he decided it would be pointless to travel down to the office first. He considered hanging about the house for another hour, but since this would certainly involve him in tying up newspapers for the weekly pickup, or washing out the garbage cans with disinfectant, or any of the other husbandly duties he did not usually mind, but did not want to be asked to do this morning, he said nothing, and left the house at his usual time, pointed virtuously towards the subway station.

He could go two ways. One way led him through upper-middle-class residential streets, across the park, and past his son's school—a pleasant, leafy stroll on a fine spring morning. But Salter was a townie; he liked shops and people and a bit of life, so he headed for the local portion of Yonge Street (the longest street in the Commonwealth), and began his stroll by walking beside the morning rush-hour traffic. He bought a paper and a cup of coffee, and sat in the mall at the entrance to the subway, enjoying the sense of playing hookey as the morning crowds poured down the stairs. When he had had his fill, he threw the paper into a bin and crossed Eglinton Avenue to walk south. He particularly liked this bit of the street, with its Chinese greengrocers, delicatessen shops, and the hardware store run by six cheerful Australians (or were they New Zealanders?) He paused at each of the three sporting-goods stores and looked at the windows, pricing the squash racquets, and he wondered again how the seven unisex hairdressers made a living. One more gas station had disappeared to make way for a fast food outlet—that made the third in the last few years. Three more restaurants had opened since he last counted, along with a shop that sold only coffee, another that sold sexy underwear, and two travel agents. Hard times? thought Salter. This town stinks of money.

At Davisville subway he turned along Chaplin Crescent into Oriole Park. Here nothing had changed in ten years. The same young mothers were watching the same babies crawl about the sandpit; the same old people were sitting on the benches; the same air-hostesses and night-workers were lying about the grass, trying to get a start on their summer tans. It was all as it was when Salter used to bring Angus and Seth here to play when Annie managed to nail him for baby-sitting on his day off. And here were the same bloody dog-owners. Salter decided to do his duty. 'You,' he called to the swaggering owner of a Doberman pinscher which was bounding about the park, preparatory to savaging one of the children. 'That your dog? Put it on a leash, and don't let it wander here again out of control.' He showed his card. 'What's its licence number?' He made a show of entering the number in his notebook. 'Right,' he said. 'Don't forget.' Across the park he saw another one, a German Shepherd, a breed he disliked and feared almost as much. He walked over to the owner, a middle-aged woman in a headscarf, standing under the trees, smoking. 'Get that dog chained up, madam,' he shouted from far enough away to justify shouting. 'There are children here and it's against the law to let your dog run wild.'

'Go to hell,' she said. 'Who are you?'

'Police Inspector,' Salter said, showing his card. 'We've had complaints. Get it under control.'

'He is under control. He wouldn't hurt a fly, unless I order him.'

The dog leaped up and took a bite at Salter's hand. 'Right,' said Salter. 'Your name, please, madam, and the dog's licence number. I'll send a man round with the charge.'

'Goddam nosey-parker,' she said. 'Why don't you clean up Yonge Street instead of bothering decent people?'

'I'm not arguing, madam. Chain it up and keep it chained up.'

'Interfering bastards,' she said. 'Here, Luba.' She got the dog on a chain and allowed herself to be hauled away, cursing through the smoke. Salter looked around, but the word had spread. All the dogs were now on leads. He went on his way satisfied, telling himself, as always, that he didn't mind the dogs, it was the owners he didn't like.

He felt much more ready to meet Mrs Summers.

Stouffville Avenue is several blocks south of the park, and Salter still had some time in hand when he arrived at Summers's house, so he strolled by it at first on the other side of the street. It seemed to him a genuine old house that had been tarted up, like so many in a district which was festooned with the signs of building renovators and architects. It was a small white house, and from the front it looked like an old cottage with a single bedroom under the roof. From the side, Salter could see that there was a new bit stuck on behind, adding at least two more rooms, one on top of the other. The front yard had been dug out and bricked in to make room for a car, even though a driveway led past the house to the back. Salter recognized the marks of a white-painter, someone who saw a perfectly good house as an opportunity to take it apart and make it into something else. He had suffered from this himself as Annie had called for more (or less) light, another bathroom, a new kitchen, and much else. Salter refused to lift a finger to help on the grounds that he was a policeman, not a carpenter, and he objected to the cost, but Annie had found the money anyway, and no longer asked him to lend a hand. The results were always pleasant, but he still fought each new suggestion bitterly.

He wondered how much Summers had done of all this, and how much he had had to put up with. Salter crossed the street and walked down the drive to the white picket fence enclosing the back yard. A woman was kneeling with her back to him, fiddling with a plant. The yard would have met with Annie's approval. Around a central grass plot were a lot of different coloured flowers, several of which looked familiar from his own back yard, a surprising number of them in bloom considering that frost was still hanging about the suburbs. The grass was littered with gardening tools. A lot of work here, thought Salter. Against the house a small patch was sown with vegetables—tomatoes and lettuce—which would ripen at the same time that they could be bought in the markets for next to nothing, the reason Salter always gave for not planting any himself.

He coughed and the woman looked up. She was thin, in early middle-age, with pretty silver hair.

'Inspector Salter,' he said.

'Yes, I know. Come in,' she said, pointing to the gate.

She threw her trowel on the grass with the rest of the tools, tossed her gloves after it, and let him in through the back door, into a kind of sunroom furnished with white wicker.

'In here,' she said. 'Do you want coffee or anything?' It was not an offer, but a request to know if it was now his coffee-hour, and was it her duty to make some.

'No, thanks,' Salter said. He waited for her to sit down before sitting opposite her.

'Would you mind if I asked you some questions about your husband?' he began.

'Ask the questions, and I'll tell you. I don't know who killed David, or why, and I don't care. It doesn't matter to me.'

This is not going to be much fun either, thought Salter. He said, 'The Montreal police have asked us to help them, and we have nothing to go on.' Salter paused. Should it be 'nothing to go on *with*? What did 'nothing to go on' mean? Would the fat chairman be interested?

Mrs Summers was waiting. Salter continued, 'He was found in a hotel room with a fractured skull, after, apparently, a good night out with his colleagues.'

'A perfect murder, then. How can I help? I was here in bed.' She was not so much hostile as indifferent, continually looking out at her garden.

'There was one clue, ma'am.'

'The killer dropped his Esso card?'

'Not quite. But there was a glass with lipstick on it in the room.'

She said nothing, as if this was no news to her, and stared at her garden.

Salter decided to give her time to respond, and he looked around, taking in the details of the room. It was agreeable and untidy: a tin of shoe-polish seemed at home on an end-table, the top of the television was a storage space for a pile of magazines, and a tea-towel hung over the back of an armchair. House and garden had the air of being left in mid-task, like the *Marie Celeste*.

Eventually she said, 'So he had a woman in his room. Who was she, do you know?'

'We don't know, ma'am.'

'Nor do I.'

'It doesn't surprise you, ma'am?'

'He was a big boy. Your age. *You* guess.'

'I'm trying to. Did he have any women friends you knew about?'

'Marika Tils. He was fond of her, all right.'

'Anyone else.'

'Not that I know of, Inspector. Last week I'd have been certain, but now I don't know. You people come across all kinds of secrets, don't you? As far as I know, or knew, David didn't have a mistress, nor did he hire prostitutes to do things I wouldn't do for him. That help?'

'That's very helpful.'

'Good. We had a fair sex life, and he had me often enough to make me pretty sure he had no one else on the side. But at your age you guys get funny, I hear. So, if you are searching for a woman, let me see, how can I help, yes, look for one with teeth marks on her.'

Salter said nothing.

She continued. 'Yes, he liked to bite—ears and neck, mostly, but he would take a nibble anywhere. Otherwise it was pretty conventional—missionary position except for Father's Day, when I got on top. I expect we had a sex life much like yours, Inspector.'

Salter said patiently, 'Did he have any enemies?'

'Nothing fierce. He sometimes called this or that colleague an asshole, to me, in private, but I expect you do that, too, eh, Inspector? He wasn't very tactful to them, either, so a lot of people were wary of him. How about you, Inspector? Are you careful of your tongue?'

'His colleagues have mentioned a feud with Professor Dunkley.'

'Oh no.' She broke her pose and sat forward. 'Oh no. Don't go off on that track. He and Dunkley were poles apart, and Dunkley *is* an asshole, but he wouldn't kill anyone. He's nasty enough to, but he couldn't justify it within his moral system or his political ethos, or whatever. Oh no. Dunkley doesn't believe in violence.'

'Then why did they dislike each other?'

She looked round the room. Then she said, 'Maybe I should make some coffee after all. I'd like some. Then I'll tell you David's life story, or the bit that matters, including the "affaire Dunkley". I feel a bit better now. I'm sorry to be rude, but this all seemed such a waste of time. David's dead and I'm trying to tell myself it was like a traffic accident. What do I care who killed him? But I can't stop thinking about him.' She got up and led the way into the kitchen which occupied the old back room of the house. Another renovation, thought Salter, noting the clear pine, the quarry tile, and the butcher's block table — all the staples of the Toronto renovated kitchen. She heated water and poured it through a filter, occupying the time while they waited for it by putting a lot of dishes in the sink and clearing the counter. Salter perched on a stool at the table and waited. She served two cups of coffee and pushed one over to him with a carton of cream and a wet spoon she fished out of the sink. She's a bit of a slob, he thought, delighted. I wonder if Summers minded? They sipped the coffee in silence for a few minutes. Then she began.

'David was nearly fifty and he was just getting used to the idea. For the last few years he had thought of himself as a failure, but he was just about through that.'

'Why a failure? He was a good enough teacher, according to one of his students, anyway.'

'Until lately he thought of himself as more than a

teacher. He was chairman of the department for a while, and after that ended he felt—what do you call it?—unfulfilled. But in the last year he had become more at home with himself. His teaching was better than ever, and he didn't care about it so much. In the past he had cared too much—a bad class could ruin his weekend and a good one would leave him flying, but he'd achieved a bit of detachment lately. He was still obsessional about it, though, preparing stuff he'd been teaching for years.'

'Was he fired as chairman?'

'Oh no. They rotate the job every three or six years. But he'd started to live and breathe it, and it was hard on him when it ended. He expected to be offered a job in the administration, and when that didn't happen he started to feel like a failure.'

'Why? Why did he expect it, and why didn't it happen?'

'His mentor quit. The vice-president David was gung-ho for took a job somewhere else, and the new one didn't like David. Simple as that. David went back to teaching, but he's only lately got used to it again.'

Salter listened, uncomfortably aware of the parallels with his own life. *This*, he thought, is the bloody Conrad story. I must tell that fat chairman one day. Thinking this brought him around to his task.

'Was it while he was chairman that he fell out with Professor Dunkley?'

'I told you, Inspector, don't bother with that one. Dunkley wouldn't hurt a fly, on principle, although he made a principle out of hating. They were opposed, of course. Those were the days of the end of the student revolution. David had a few confrontations, and dug down deep in his heart and discovered he was a wishy-washy liberal who believed the students were entitled to run everything except the classroom. Dunkley was involved in all of the sit-ins and supported the students' right to decide everything—including what they should be taught. There was an incident almost every day and those two were always on opposite sides.' She paused, and looked as though she were gathering energy for the rest of it. 'But that wasn't the whole of it. You see—oh, shit—about that time Dunkley became separated from his wife, and just shortly thereafter David and Dunkley's wife became lovers, and Dunkley found out, and they didn't talk to each other after that, even though, according to Dunkley's principles, his wife was free to do what she liked. OK? Now you know it all.'

'How did you hear of it?'

'David is a poor liar. Sorry, "was", so I would have found out soon enough, but in this case Dunkley's wife told him, to spite him, I think—poor Dunkley, no one likes him—and Dunkley told me.'

And that was the end of that, thought Salter. But it gave Dunkley all the motive in the world. He returned to pick at his own new-found relationship with Summers. The parallel fascinated him.

'Why did he seem better lately?' he asked. 'What made the difference?'

'You probably know the answer, Inspector, or you will. How old are you?'

Startled, Salter told her.

'David was nearly fifty. We have some money now, and we were beginning to get around more. Travel. There was no need for him to spend all his time upstairs at his desk, though he still did, most of the winter. But we went away at Christmas, and for a few weeks during the summer.' She looked at him calmly. 'Our sex life improved, and he started to have some fun. He even began to write poetry—no good, but nice. He took up the bits of adolescence he never had, and finished off growing up.'

Salter got annoyed. 'Why does it have to be adolescent?

Maybe he just enjoyed playing squash.'

'Don't get uptight about it, Inspector. You didn't even know him. I think everyone walks around with every age inside him, especially adolescence, but some people get a chance to let the other ages out—the lucky ones.'

This sounded to Salter like one of those conversations that end up discussing whether we are all faggots, really, if only we would relax, and he cut her off.

'You had no money worries?' he asked.

'Nope.' She pointed to the ceiling. 'The house is paid for. Our daughter is nearly through college, and I'm making money. I work for an agency. We find new jobs for executives who have been fired or want to quit. I'm good at it and I make a lot of money. I wanted to help David—I could have slotted him into a new career without any trouble, but he wouldn't allow me near him on that one.'

Bloody right, thought Salter.

'And David was making money himself, on the side,' she added.

'How?'

'On the futures market. It was another thing Dunkley didn't like about him. He called David a capitalist. Silly prick. David was a *gambler* in a modest sort of way. He was watching TV one day and saw a commodities broker who impressed him as a man who knew where it was at. The next day he phoned the broker and opened an account. It's a kind of betting on the future prices of things. David had tried the stock market, but that's rigged in favour of the brokers and the insiders, he said. He had spent a year playing the stock market and earned ten thousand in commissions for the broker and five hundred for himself. This commodities thing was different. He had a good trader—a woman, by the way—and she made him some money. He took back his original stake in six months—I think he put fifteen thousand in originally—and he's been playing with his winnings ever since. Right now he was in cotton, copper and the Swiss franc.

'But Dunkley didn't understand anything about it. He thought that if you made a bet on the future price of pork bellies you were playing with the food of the poor. Even if you lost your shirt. I warn you, Inspector, if you ever get into the futures market, don't tell anyone. They'll be jealous and righteous if you win, and bloody happy if you lose. Which reminds me. I should find out what is happening to us. It's a joint account and all our accounts were frozen until the will is probated, but the positions can still change. Excuse me.' She went to the phone and dialled a number which she read off a list pasted above the receiver. 'Leslie Stone, please. This is Mrs Summers, David's wife. Thank you. I just wondered how we were doing. Good. Thanks. I'll be in touch as soon as they unfreeze things.' She hung up and came back to the table. 'David trusted her totally,' she said. 'Apparently we are making money today.'

Salter was struck with an idea. 'Would you call her again,' he asked, 'and authorize her to speak to me?'

'Why?'

'I'll tell you if I'm right. I just had an idea.'

'OK. Hang on.' She dialled and spoke once more to the broker, and handed the phone to Salter. The broker's voice was cheery with a touch of metal in it 'Hi there, Inspector,' she said. 'What's up?'

'Probably nothing, ma'am. There are some questions around Mr Summers's death, that's all.'

'I won't be much good. I never even knew what he looked like.'

'You never saw him, *ever*?'

'Nope. I'll miss him, though. He was an easy client.'

'How so?'

'He never cried when he lost. Some of my clients cry the

house down every time they lose a thousand dollars.'

Christ, so would I, lady. 'Can you remember the last time you talked to him?'

'Sure, last Friday when he called from Montreal.'

'Did you do any business then?'

'No. We didn't buy anything or sell anything. I had some good news for him, though. He made two thousand dollars that day.'

'How?'

'On the sovereignty referendum. He bought two Canadian dollars, and when the sovereignty results came in he had made a full cent.'

'Two cents?'

'A thousand dollars a cent. A hundred points.'

'I see. He bought two hundred thousand dollars the day before and now they were worth two hundred and two thousand. Right?'

'That's right, Inspector. More or less.'

'That's a lot of money, isn't it?'

'It's two contracts.'

'He must have had over two hundred thousand dollars on deposit with you?' Salter saw Mrs Summers smiling to herself.

'Inspector, I'm very busy, but I'll give you a short course in commodity trading. To buy a hundred thousand Canadian dollars you only have to put up thirty-five hundred, the amount you might lose in a bad week, say. David used seven thousand, or about half of his equity on those two contracts. He was one of our teeny-weeny accounts. If everything went bad he could lose the lot in three days.'

'Could he, by Christ. But this time he won?'

'That's right. And you know why he was so happy? He did it himself. I advised against it and he always took our advice, but this time he wanted to make a bet on his own. I can't get it up for the Canadian dollar, but he was sure of this one. He was happy as hell when he won. I'll miss him.'

'Thank you very much, Miss Stone.'

'OK, Boss.'

Salter had a thought. 'By the way, if I wanted to get in on this, would you take me on?'

'Sure. We've upped the ante, though. You'd need a bit more cash.'

'How much?'

'Seventy-five thousand would get you started. A hundred would be better.'

'Thanks.' Salter hung up, and returned to his chair. 'That clears up David's lucky day,' he said. David? Since when did the corpse have a first name? This was all getting a shade cosy.

Mrs Summers said, 'He's won that much before. I wonder why he made such a big deal of it? Still, that's it, then. End of mystery. Would you like some lunch, Inspector? I could make some scrambled eggs.'

Salter shook himself. 'No, thanks, ma'am. I have work to do. I know now about his lucky day, and I also know about one of the phone calls—it was to her, the broker.' He felt the wallet in his pocket, and handed it to her. 'Your husband's wallet, Mrs Summers. Would you check it, and give me a receipt for it? We've photostated everything in it.'

She took it gingerly, and turned it over. Then she laid out the contents on the table and checked them against the itemized list that formed the receipt. 'Money, credit cards, driver's licence, charge slips, receipts, lottery tickets—I'll have to check those, I suppose—library cards, squash club membership. Here you go, Inspector,' she scribbled her name, and put the wallet in a wicker basket full of bills and unanswered mail. 'I'll look at it all later.' There was a pause. The interview seemed over, but Salter did not feel like going immediately.

She sensed this, and asked, 'More coffee? Might as well finish it.'

Salter put out his cup. 'Was your husband reading a paper in Montreal?' he asked, by way of keeping things going.

'Oh no. He didn't go to Montreal to read papers. I don't think many of them do. David just wanted to see if there was anything left of Baghdad there.'

'Baghdad?'

'A family joke. David coined it with a friend one day when they were talking about travel. His friend said that he had never wasted a dollar he spent on travel, and David felt the same way. But he was always looking for a Baghdad to travel to. Baghdad was the place, the mysterious city—always a city—where things were new and strange, the place where something interesting could happen to you. Paris was Baghdad. David had been several times and it turned him on so much he hardly went to bed. He used to wander round meeting people, finding himself in places, letting things happen to him. New York was Baghdad, so was San Francisco. Some places stopped being Baghdads before you got around to them—Dublin was one of those. He wanted to go to Dublin for years, and then he didn't. Other places were Baghdads once, but not the second or third time. London was one of those. Well, Montreal used to be a Baghdad and he wondered if there was anything left of it.'

Salter asked delicately, 'Did you go with him to these Baghdads?'

'Yes and no. We went to New York together—I have to go sometimes on business, but though we had a great time, it wasn't Baghdad when I was around. I think he got a bit of it in the daytime when I was busy. The only place I know of that was Baghdad when I was with him was Corfu.'

'So part of Baghdad is being alone?'

'Sure. Some part of it was the lovely dark-haired lady who beckoned from the doorway. That's why he liked to take a trip by himself once a year, even to an academic conference. You could always keep your eyes open for Baghdad.'

'Mrs Summers, are you telling me that he might have found a bit of Baghdad in Montreal, and she killed him?'

'No, Inspector. It's possible, but unlikely. I'm just saying that Baghdad was a romantic fantasy, and at the right age it includes sex. But it didn't have to, and for the last twenty years it probably didn't. To come down to earth, David would not have found anything interesting or mysterious about a Montreal whore. Anyway the idea of David in bed with a prostitute anywhere is absurd, unless he had spent the previous six months in the Arctic, and not even then, probably. He would never have been happy in bed except with someone who liked him. It's just—well, there are no whores in Baghdad. Am I making sense?'

Too much, thought Salter.

'Thank you, Mrs Summers,' he said formally. 'You have been very helpful.' He finished his coffee and stood up. 'One last thing. One of his colleagues told me your husband kept a journal, a diary. I didn't find it in the office. Have you come across it? If so, may I look at it? There's always the chance that he may have been involved in something he told no one else about, not even you. But he might have put something in a diary.'

She laughed and got up. 'I read it last night.' She took a thick notebook from the wicker basket where she had put the wallet. It seemed to be her filing system. 'Here. Nothing very scandalous or embarrassing in it. Maybe it will give you some ideas of him. Have a look at it, but bring it back, please.'

He put it in his pocket and moved to shake hands as he left, but suddenly overcome, she shook her head and pushed him through the door without speaking. He left the house and headed for the Kensington Market, where he was meeting Molly for lunch. Baghdad.

She was waiting for him, seated at an outside table of a café specializing in health foods. She had on the same jeans and T-shirt as before.

'Hi, Charlie,' she called when he was fifty yards away, making him slightly self-conscious. He habitually wore a tweed jacket and grey flannel trousers, even in summer—these were the casual clothes of his youth, and he was stuck in them—and on this day he had added an open-necked sports shirt instead of a shirt and tie because he wanted to change easily at the squash club. He had felt very informal talking to Mrs Summers, but in these surroundings he felt like a banker. All round them the counter-culture was on display; most of the people were under thirty, dressed in blankets and sacking. At one table a boy sat with his eyes closed and his hands in the air, making two circles with thumbs and forefingers. Meditating? At another, two young mothers tented in curtains were demonstrating the joys of breast-feeding to the passers-by.

'Have a fellafel burger,' Molly suggested.

Salter looked at the menu but could recognize nothing, and he shrugged and nodded. When it arrived it turned out to be a giant sesame-seed bun filled with weeds and roots. Salter found it tasty.

'I'm having mint tea,' Molly said. 'They do have coffee for addicts,' she said.

'That's me. Coffee with extra caffein, please, and two spoonfuls of white, cancer-inducing sugar.' You've got to stand up for your own, he thought.

After the food she sat looking expectant, like a good student. Salter began, 'I'd like to know about the other teachers at Douglas. How did Summers compare, as a teacher, with the others in the department that you had?'

'I only had two others. Dunkley taught me Canadian Literature, and a man named Philpott, an Englishman, taught American Lit. He's not there now.'

'What happened to him? What are you smiling about?'

'He left in mid-term and Professor Browne, the chairman, finished the course.' She laughed. 'Philpott never turned up much and we complained about him. A lot. We called him the Great Canadian Doctor.'

'Why?'

'It turned out he was a fake, no degree, nothing. By rights, according to the proper rules of fiction, he should have been brilliant, but he was a joke. When he did come to class, about once a week, he used to read book reviews to us that he'd got from the library. Browne hushed it up and everybody passed the course.'

'And Dunkley?'

'He's OK. He is supposed to be very left-wing and he wears all the gear, but he's really an old-fashioned schoolmaster. He made us work. In theory you could choose your own way of passing his course, but by the time you had finished discussing it with him you had already done more work than you would have done in a conventional course. He made you do your own course outline, and to do that properly you had to know all the material before you started.'

Salter had run out of questions.

'Anything else?' she asked brightly.

'I guess not. I don't suppose I'll have to bother you again.'

'Hardly worth meeting for, was it? Or was it just an excuse?'

'It was just an excuse. I wanted to see you,' he said nervously.

'That's nice. Do you want to see me again?'

Salter floundered. She rescued him. 'I'm not

propositioning you, Charlie. But we can get together if you like.'

But, Salter thought, you are twenty years old and I am forty-six and you cannot have any idea of how foolish I feel. Summers may have liked your essays as well, but he must have enjoyed you as much as I do.

'I may need your help later on,' he said, dodging.

'You don't have to need my help. Just call me. Or I'll call you—for a beer.'

'No, don't do that.'

'I see. Your wife would mind?'

That didn't take much thought. 'Yes.'

'Don't worry. I won't let you do anything silly.'

The middle-aged police inspector who had seen everything smiled shyly. 'All right,' he said. 'It's nice to see how the rest of the world lives.'

'Isn't it? Now I have to go. Are you buying my lunch? You won't feel compromised?'

'No. I'll put it on expenses, then I'll know it was business. I'm still conducting an investigation.'

'Good.' She touched his hand. 'Finish your coffee.' She walked away, threading between the tables, waving at him as she reached the kerb. Salter hunched happily over the dregs of his coffee.

Salter changed into his old tennis clothes, and wondered what to do with his valuables. The attendant showed him a row of little wooden cubby-holes with locks, and Salter chose one and deposited his wallet and watch, putting the elastic wristlet with the key in his pocket in preference to wearing it. The pro was waiting for him on the court.

'Like this,' the pro said. He dropped the ball on to his racquet and hit it against the front wall of the court. Salter swung at it and missed. 'And again,' the pro said. Swing and hit, with the handle. 'And again.' Swing and hit, straight up to the ceiling. 'That's it,' the pro said. 'I can see you've played a lot of tennis.' Salter smirked. They kept at it for ten minutes, sometimes keeping the ball in play for as much as four successive hits. Then the pro suggested a rally. 'Just keep the ball in play,' he said. Ten minutes later Salter thought it was all up with him. His lungs were heaving, his heart pounded in his ears, and he could barely see for the sweat. 'How's your condition?' the pro asked. He had gooseflesh from the chilly court.

Salter took a deep breath. 'And again,' he sobbed, and hit the ball hard, and properly.

'Terrific,' said the pro, and returned it from behind his back without looking.

At the end Salter said, 'I want another lesson tomorrow.' They left the court and Salter walked down the corridor to the changing-room which was now crowded. He took his clothes off, feeling ill at ease among a lot of nude lawyers, self-conscious about his varicose veins and his old gall-bladder scar. But under the shower, and then, in the whirlpool, he forgot himself in the pleasure of having stretched his body.

He dressed and waited in the lounge, and soon Bailey appeared for his game with Cranmer, the accountant. He dropped his eyes when he noticed Salter, then looked up very quickly and greeted the inspector with a lot of noise. 'How's it going, chief?' was one of the things he said.

'I've just had my first lesson,' Salter said. 'I think I'll join.'

'Really? Maybe we'll have a game, sometime.'

'When I've had a couple more lessons.'

They sat quiet then, waiting for each other to speak. Bailey broke first. 'Any news on Old Dave?' he asked.

'None. I'll tell you, Mr Bailey, we are baffled. It looks as though it must have been a casual set-up.'

'He got rolled, you think?'

'Something like that.'

'Poor old Dave, eh? Well, I'd better change. Percy is always on time.' He bustled about with his racquet and bag.

'One thing, Mr Bailey. I was just checking on a few odds and ends. Summers made a couple of calls from Montreal on Friday afternoon . . .'

'That's right, Inspector, I forgot to tell you. One of them was to me, to tell me he couldn't play squash the next Monday. He'd forgotten to tell me when I saw him on Thursday that he was going to Montreal for this conference.'

'I see. That was all, was it? Did he sound very excited?'

Bailey considered this. 'Excited? No, I wouldn't say he sounded any different from his usual self. No.'

'Why would he phone to cancel a game if you hadn't arranged it?'

'Oh, it was a standard arrangement we had. We only got in touch when we couldn't make it. Otherwise my secretary booked the courts for us every day.'

'I see. It must have been an exciting game on that Thursday to make him forget.'

'Yeah. We always went at it pretty hard. That it, then? Here's Percy now.'

Bailey and Cranmer went off to the changing-rooms and Salter went in search of the manager to make preliminary enquiries about joining the club. Once he had started the process, he decided to go ahead and become a member there and then.

CHAPTER 6

The next morning Salter woke with the thought that one of his many enemies had finally caught up with him in an alley. As well as having two broken legs, he had obviously been worked over from the neck down. So this is what it feels like, he thought. Then he remembered the cause and began to enjoy his pain, the product of his first serious exercise in ten years. He had slept like an athlete, too, and he lay there, thinking of the day before, and watching the stirrings of his wife who slept high on her pillow, her waist almost level with his face. It was seven o'clock and Salter watched her dig deeper into the pillow for a few extra minutes. He waited until she was still again, then he peeled the duvet back, lifted up her nightdress, and bit her gently on the bottom.

She didn't move. 'What's this?' she asked.

'Bum-biting,' he said. 'A traditional arousal technique. I thought I'd try it.'

'Like it?'

'Not much.'

'Good.'

'Want me to try something else?'

She turned and lay on her back. 'I'm not terrifically in the mood,' she said. 'But you are. So how about a Victorian quickie.' She pulled her nightdress up around her waist.

'Right,' he said and rolled towards her. 'Aaaargh, Holy Christ. I can't move. Aaaargh. I played squash yesterday. I can't move.'

'What a vicious circle,' she said. 'You play squash to get fit to improve your sex life, and now you can't move. OK. When you are convalescent, let me know.' She stepped out of bed and into the bathroom.

He lay back among his aches. 'You'll pay for this,' he shouted. 'I'll walk again, you'll see.' After a while he clambered slowly out of bed and edged into his dressing-gown. Downstairs, some minutes later, he met the wondering stare of his two sons, who had heard him shouting and now watched him limping about the kitchen.

The hell with them, he thought. Let them wonder.

He forgot his pain the instant the pro hit the ball to start his second lesson later that morning. This time he hit the ball nearly every time, even essaying some rudimentary placing and shot-making. 'Wow!' the pro said, between looking at his watch. This time the lesson cost him ten dollars for half an hour.

'Found a motive, yet, Charlie?' Harry Wycke stood in the door of Salter's office as he got ready to leave for Montreal.

'You want to hear about it, Harry? I've got a few minutes before I leave.'

'Sure.' Wycke sat down on the hard little visitor's chair and looked around the office. 'Not exactly top-of-line here, is it?' he said.

'It's what they had left over.' Was Wycke about to patronize him?

But the detective just shrugged, and waited for him to speak.

Salter summarized the story so far, and Wycke listened carefully.

'What next?' he asked, when Salter had finished.

'I'm going down to Montreal this afternoon to have a look round. You have any advice?'

Wycke shook his head. 'I wouldn't look for anything complicated. Sex. Money. Both.' He stood up. 'Want me to check out the bookies here? See if he was known to be over his head?'

'Yes, thanks, Harry. But I can't see it.'

'Nor can I. But it's an obvious one, so we'll cover your ass on it.' He winked and left.

The afternoon train from Toronto to Montreal takes a little less than five hours. Salter carried along Summers's

journal to pass the time, hoping, in spite of Mrs
Summers, to find it interesting as well as useful. He
treated himself to the first-class section so that he could
drink beer and read in comfort, and was assigned a seat
by the window; ideal, because, although there is nothing
worth looking at on the Montreal-Toronto journey,
staring out the window, or appearing to, was the easiest
way of avoiding conversation with the other passengers.

The first few pages of the journal depressed him. It was
declared immediately that this was Summers's first
exercise in journal-keeping, and the early pages consisted
of a long, rambling, 'literary' account of the author's
condition—mental, physical, psychological, sexual (too
coy to be interesting), social, paternal, marital, fraternal,
spiritual ('I know, finally, that I must die;' for Christ's
sake, thought Salter), and professional. Salter thumbed
through the first hundred pages. About thirty pages in,
Summers had written: 'Joyce feeling larky today, and we
had a nice time before we got up this morning.' This was
more like it. Salter ordered a beer and settled back with
page one.

Gradually as he read on, Summers's life emerged from
his literary concern with the writing of the journal. The
entries grew shorter—soon a page was a long entry—and
the journal came alive as it became a record of what was
happening to Summers rather than a collection of
pensées. It began with an enquiry into the writer's
depressed state. He was sleeping badly, waking up
anxious, and savouring little, it seemed. Salter recognized
the condition as his own and reflected that it was
probably widespread, normal, and boring. What was
more interesting was the upward movement of the
journal, marked by the disappearance of introspection,
and Salter read more closely to see how Summers had
come out of it. The appearance of his new hobby, squash,
was the first sign that Summers had gone beyond his

fascination with his own melancholy to doing something about it. After about two months, Summers began to mention his games regularly, especially those with Cranmer and Bailey. Soon Cranmer faded, but the games with Bailey were regularly recorded, together with comments. Once Summers wrote: 'Exhausted. Played Bailey today — beat him — he wanted to play again — beat him again. Almost felt sorry for him, and offered to buy the beer. He got very snotty about it. Said I would be buying the beer soon enough. Ho. Ho. I look forward to it all day. We are dead even, but I am feeling up this week. Sometimes I feel a bit embarrassed about this new obsession, but there's a distinguished professor over at the U. of T. who doesn't give a shit for anything except his horse.' A later entry read: 'Lost to Bailey today. My eye still black from last week. I think he's been taking lessons, too.' During a squash tournament, apparently among the 'D' players at the club, the journal stopped for ten days, and Salter reflected that this kind of journal was probably only kept up when the writer felt sad.

Sometimes Summers reprimanded himself for not keeping it conscientiously. The first entry of this kind occurred about a third of the way through, and was the result of Summers himself having read the first six months of his journal and having found it fascinating. Food appeared occasionally as Summers described the meals he had eaten in restaurants, along with the prices. Here, too, he was beginning to see the interest such information might have for him in the future. Sometimes he recorded the movies and plays he had seen and included a considered, literary reaction. More to Salter's taste was: 'Saw a lot of frauds farting around the stage of the St Lawrence Centre last night', and 'Fell asleep during concert yesterday. Drooled a bit, but no one noticed.'

Douglas College was a major theme. All the 'great' classes as well as the total failures were recorded — there

seemed to be about one of each a week. Then, among the
more detailed comments on the classes, Salter began to
detect the figure of Molly Tripp. She was called by name,
in the last fifty pages, but Salter recognized her very early
as 'a nice girl in the second row with curly hair and blue
jeans.' She appeared several times as someone who 'saved'
a class on Wordsworth or someone, just as it was
collapsing. Then she turned up at the office to talk about
an essay. Soon she was identified as Molly Tripp, and
Summers started having coffee with her. He wondered
(but not to her) if she always wore blue jeans. Then he
wondered it again. In the second term, about half way
through the journal, she turned into plain Molly, and
Summers indulged in a mild, erotic fantasy. 'Just once,'
he wrote 'I'd like to see her without her jeans on. (Maybe,
though, she has wizened or hairy legs, like Geraldine.)'
Salter wondered who the hell the unfortunate Geraldine
was—one of Summers's relatives? Significantly enough,
Molly turned into 'M'. Summers never took the final step
into real intimacy in the journal, seeming always to be
wary of an eye over his shoulder, but the adoption of the
initial was surely a sign of his heightened, illicit interest in
the girl. ' "M" came,' he wrote, 'and I managed to keep
her for an hour. Next week she is going to have a beer
with me.' Then came the lie. 'Without a few students like
her, this job would be impossible,' clearly to assure an
outsider (reassure his wife?) of his proper interest in
Molly.

The beer did not take place, and Summers's other
interest in the girl never was spoken between them. She
appeared twice before the exams to chat, and Summers
wondered if she saw more in him than a teacher. She
came after the exam to say she had enjoyed the course,
and Summers wrote: 'So I told her about her "A". She was
as pleased as I was. Hung around a long time, but I

couldn't make anything out of it. Does she know what's going on?'

That was the last of Molly. By watching her progress and guessing at the degree of emotion involved, Salter was able to make sense of some of the relationships of the other characters to the journalist. Joyce Summers occurred regularly, usually in reference to some outing they had enjoyed. There appeared to be no serious fighting, but often a day or two of squabbling, usually resolved by, in Summers's phrase, 'a nice lay'. Summers was mostly pleased with his wife. Marika Tils was his confidant. She interpreted his dreams, cheered him up after bad classes, and gossiped with him about their colleagues. She never came to the house, apparently, but Slater decided that the fact that she was fully identified meant that they had no sexual interest in each other. Two other initials cropped up from time to time. A woman identified as 'S' was the subject of romantic fantasies; the two had lunch sometimes, but there was nothing urgent about their affair, if such it was. Apparently Summers fancied himself in love with her and enjoyed the idea without any impulse to lose the world for her. In the references to 'S', Summers's literary spark glowed again, but without much heat.

In the last third of the journal Summers began to record his new interest in the commodities market. He was fascinated by the possibility of making his fortune, and every weekend he calculated the week's profit or loss. As Mrs Summers had said, he did surprisingly well. The last entry concerned the Montreal conference. 'Looking forward to Thursday. Have not been to Montreal for ten years. J. coming. Our fifth anniversary.'

Salter put the journal back in his bag and ordered a third and last beer. The train was passing through Cornwall. Who was J? Who else but the Dean of Women? The journal held no other surprises, in form or content, but there was one omission that puzzled Salter. The entries about his colleagues were rare enough; mainly they concerned Marika Tils, although the others were mentioned here and there, usually in connection with departmental politics, all except Dunkley who was not mentioned once. Salter wondered: If 'D' is more significant than Dunkley, as indicating a higher degree of emotional involvement, was the omission of D even more significant? They must have hated each other.

O'Brien was waiting at the terminus to take him in hand. He was dressed in a sports shirt with an insect embroidered on the pocket, and a pair of white trousers. Salter couldn't resist it. 'You look like an RCMP narcotics agent,' he said.

O'Brien made a face. 'We are going out on the town, Charlie. I am trying to look like a Toronto professor in search of a piece of French tail.'

'That, too,' Salter said comfortingly. O'Brien's Volkswagen was illegally parked in the taxi-rank outside the terminus, and they drove off after he had thrown away the ticket he had acquired.

'How are the plans for St Jean Baptiste day coming? Need any help?' Salter asked as they drove along.

'You know about our cultural festivities, eh?'

'I know somebody threw a Coke bottle at Trudeau one year. Are you expecting any excitement this time?'

'Fireworks. Real ones. We could use a couple of hundred mounted police. You have influence?'

'There's just me and Frank. He's got piles and I can't ride.'

'You should learn how. Then when Québec separates you could join the cavalry and lead the charge down Highway 401.'

'No good. Your road is so bad we would never get across the border.'

'Ha, ha, ha. Are you finished with the jokes, Charlie? Can I talk about the case? Something has cropped up.'

'OK. Go ahead.'

'Summers used two keys to his room. You remember we found two keys.'

'Right. He took one when he checked in, left it in his room by mistake, and needed another one to get in when he came home that night.'

'No one remembers him asking for the second key. This is not a busy hotel, Charlie. They would have noticed.'

'But they didn't.'

'He didn't ask for a second key. I've been talking to the clerks again. The one who checked Summers in remembers somebody asking for a second key that afternoon.'

'So he forgot it right away. What is this, Onree? Why are you picking at this?'

'Those two keys bothered me. Now, listen.'

Salter sighed. He enjoyed O'Brien, but if he was one of those people who say 'listen', their friendship would wither quickly. 'Yes,' he said. 'I'm listening.'

'OK. Now. This same desk clerk remembers someone—it could have been Summers—giving him an envelope to put in another mailbox. The envelope had something in it which could have been a hotel key.'

'Was it a key or not, Onree?'

'Of course it was. This clerk doesn't want us to know that he goes through the mail and shakes all the envelopes. You know. A pointed-nose one.'

'So Summers left his key in someone's mailbox. Case complete. Whose?'

'Jane Homer's. The clerk knew because she wrote a note for Summers.'

'The one we got.'

'Yes. It must be.'

'He didn't read the note?'

'No. He says not.'

'Look, Onree, why don't you pour a litre of olive oil down his throat to start with, then staple his ears to his head, then put his testicles in a garlic press, one by one. Maybe he will remember what was in the note and who sent it to who.'

'We can't do that here, Charlie.'

'We do it all the time, only we use nut-crackers because there's no garlic in Ontario.'

'This is very droll, Inspector, but I thought it was important.'

Salter took warning. 'Sorry, Onree. I woke up feeling good, but it's wearing off. All right, so he left a key for Jane Homer to let herself in. I'll talk to her again. She's no killer, though.'

'Did she admit she was in his room?'

'She said she never saw him.'

'When will you talk to her?'

'As soon as I get back. If I learn anything interesting I'll call you.'

By now they had crossed the centre of Montreal.

'I've booked you in Summers's hotel,' O'Brien said. 'We will retrace his footsteps.' He had driven them neatly through the rush-hour traffic to the Hotel Plaza del Oro, and parked in the hotel lot. As they went through the front doors, O'Brien said, 'This is the main entrance, but as you see, the killer did not have to come through here.' The front desk was directly in line with the door, but on either side of the lobby there were smaller doors exiting on to the street. 'You see, he could have walked through that door and stepped straight into the elevator. No one would stop him. I have already registered you so we can go right up to your room.'

The room was standard North American middle class. Two large beds, a television set, two chairs, five coffee tables, and a closet big enough to take twenty suits of clothes. Also a bathroom with an extra coloured lamp in the ceiling which soaked you in ultra-violet light while you were sitting on the toilet.

Salter was wearing his sports jacket, and in deference to his colleague, he took off his tie and put his pen in his inside pocket. 'The best I can do,' he said.

'You look like a Toronto professor who has forgotten to put his tie on,' O'Brien said.

'I could comb my hair forward.'

'Don't worry. Together, we are hard to read, I'm sure. Now. This is it. Every room is identical. Summers had one on the next floor up.'

'Show me how it looked.'

O'Brien arranged the chairs. 'Like this. Two chairs opposite each other. Summers on the floor. Blood everywhere. The whisky bottle here. One glass here. Over here, his suitcase, open but unpacked. Here, by the bed, his clothes, in a heap. The bed was not touched. He had took off his clothes and sat drinking in the chair, I think. The newspaper was here.'

That's the first English mistake he's made, thought Salter.

'It looks as though he was expecting someone, and that's all we know,' O'Brien concluded.

'We know he was expecting Jane Homer. But who else?'

The men stared around the room for a few minutes, then O'Brien said, 'Let's go to the college.'

They left the hotel and walked for two blocks until they came to the building where the Learned Societies meeting was still going on. The French teachers were currently in session—the whole conference took several weeks to run through all the disciplines—and Salter and O'Brien were able to look over the scene of the conference very much as it had been when Summers was killed.

O'Brien said, 'Summers arrived, spent some time in his hotel room, then probably walked to the conference in time to go to the bar after the last session of the day, at four-thirty.'

They passed through the main doors into a crowd of delegates with name tags, standing about in groups. O'Brien led them along a corridor to a bar, a converted classroom, just opening for business.

'This is where he first appeared, Onree?'

'Yes. The others met him here, and they had a drink and went off to dinner.'

The two men looked around. They were learning nothing.

'I didn't put out a request for information,' O'Brien said. 'There were thousands who might have seen him, but if anyone had anything to tell us they would have come forward. That is what the Chairman of the Association thinks, and I agree.'

They walked outside and turned back towards the hotel, along the Rue St Denis, and Salter thought: How bloody easily they do it here. The sidewalk cafés were designed for sitting outside in the summer, and both sides of the street were lined with tables, filled mostly with students drinking beer. Compared to this, Salter thought, in Toronto, for a price, you could sit on two feet of pavement stolen from the sidewalk. Why? Why did they build the sidewalks like this in Montreal and like that in Toronto? The climate was the same. Was it part of the difference between England and France, between London and Paris?

'Let's have a beer,' he said. 'Here. We've got some time to spare.'

They sat down and Salter took in the scene. Baghdad?

The Maison Victor Hugo was two blocks away, a converted house with a small painted sign over the door to indicate its present business. Inside, a table was waiting for them by the small window, and O'Brien placed his colleague so that he could see the street.

'They had that table,' O'Brien said, pointing to one in the centre of the room. 'The waiter remembers them because they were having such a good time.'

'*Bonjour, Monsieur Sergeant.*' The manager was standing by his table. He spoke some more in French.

In English, O'Brien replied. 'I'm off duty tonight. My friend from Toronto is in town and I have brought him here to preserve the reputation of the city. Monsieur Salter,' he added as an introduction.

The manager bowed, shook hands, and spoke again in French. He bowed again and left.

'What was that?' Salter asked.

'He said, "Have a good time and enjoy your meal." If you come here on your own you should buy a phrasebook, Charlie.'

'I know. Especially if you separate.'

'Oh, if we separate it won't matter. We can speak our language and you can speak yours. It is having to speak yours that pisses us off.'

'O'Brien isn't French, Onree. Why do you say "we"?'

' "We" means "Québécois". My name is Irish from my great-grandfther who was a labourer on the railroad. He met my great-grandmother when he was working on a repair gang near Saint Agathe. He settled down, went native, became a Québécois. He was Catholic already, so it was easy. What about you? "Thank God I'm English," and all that?'

'My father's family were, yes. My mother didn't know what she was. She came over as a domestic servant, sent by an English orphanage. I grew up in Cabbagetown, like your St Henri, then—but we moved out of it after the war because it got too slummy, even for us. Now it's very trendy.'

'How do you know about St Henri?'

'*The Tin Flute*. We did it in college.'

The waiter appeared, flourishing a pen. Salter let his host do the ordering, and they ate some carrot soup, a veal stew that tasted agreeably of liquorice, and a big piece of soft, white cheese with some strawberries. They ate a lot of bread with it and drank a big bottle of wine. Salter was not a connoisseur, but he had eaten enough bad food to know the good when he tasted it, even if the upper levels of discrimination were beyond him. This all tasted all right.

'How much, Onree?' he asked at the end.

'My check . . .'

'All right, but how much? Summers spent a hundred and thirty dollars here on five dinners.'

O'Brien picked up the check. 'Thirty-eight dollars. They must have drunk a lot of wine. OK, Charlie, let's see what's next on the agenda.' O'Brien paid the bill, leaving what seemed to Salter a huge tip. Salter used the washroom before they left, and was pleased with himself for being able to translate the slogan above the urinal — '*A bas les anglais.*' He wondered if he could still pee that high, and the thought was father to the deed. Just a short burst, but enough to satisfy.

They began with a cognac at the outdoor café next door. Now the street was full of strollers, cyclists, and people drinking. Students sat in windows on the second stories, calling to their friends on the street as the curtain rose on a perfect evening in early summer in the quarter.

'And now to the first bar,' O'Brien said. They walked south, to a sign which announced simply, '*Danseuses*'. Inside, an ordinary bar counter ran from the door along one wall. The rest of the long room was filled with tables and chairs. The two men sat at a table near the bar and ordered beer.

'They came here first and had one drink. Summers was still paying,' O'Brien said.

Behind the bar a middle-aged couple filled the orders,

and chatted between drinks with a similar middle-aged couple seated at the bar. The scene was domestic and suburban, except for the bare breasts of the waitresses. Then, at the far end of the room, a spotlight lit up one of the tables, and a waitress climbed on the table and took off her skirt. Underneath she was naked. It was still early in the evening, and there were only about a dozen people in the room. The patrons all got up from their tables and moved closer to the girl who was wiggling in time to the juke-box. She jigged for about three minutes while the drinkers watched, then she jumped down, put her skirt on and began taking orders for drinks. Her place was taken by the other waitress who put herself in a back arch on all fours and walked around on the table in this position, like a giant crab.

O'Brien and Salter stayed where they were by the bar in spite of polite urgings by the bar-tender to move closer.

O'Brien saw Salter taking in the whole room, and said, 'They are not here, are they?'

'Who?'

'The whores. The muggers. The hoods.'

Salter confessed that he had been looking for them, and that the room was utterly without any sign of the lower depths. Except for the nudity, it might have been Monday night at the Canadian Legion.

'*Allons*,' O'Brien said. 'The next one is more lively.'

They crossed the street and walked south for a block until they came to a store-front whose windows were covered with posters advertising '*nus*'.

'Les Jardins du Paradis,' O'Brien said.

They pushed a cloth curtain aside and were met by a youth sitting at a card-table. 'Two dollars, messieurs,' he said. 'And two dollars for me if you want a good seat.'

'*Bonjour, Paul*,' O'Brien said. The youth looked up. '*Ah. Monsieur le detective. Encore*. For you a good table is free but it is still two dollars to get in.' He stood up and

guided them through a second curtain into the main body
of the old store. Once more the scene was simple. A small
stage of planks about ten feet square was set up against
one wall. Around it and filling up the room were plastic
tables, each with four chairs, which were mostly
occupied. The boy led them to a table right by the stage,
one which the waitresses used to rest their trays between
orders. He set a couple of drinks at it, and the two men
sat down.

The crowd was young, young enough to make Salter
feel self-conscious. Although there were more men than
women, there were plenty of couples in the room. Salter
ordered beer from a waitress and was amazed to find it
cost no more than it should. The music began and the
routine at the first bar was repeated. Their waitress was
first, and she performed a brisk striptease for about ten
minutes. During the first song, she took off her skirt and
pants; during the second she unhooked her brassiere;
finally her underpants came off and she shook herself
vigorously for two or three minutes with an absent-
minded air, like someone doing her morning exercises
while thinking of the day ahead. The effect was to make
Salter feel he had nothing to fear by way of
embarrassment from these girls.

The next dancer ended that. Some quieter music
began, and a girl ran up on stage in jeans and a T-shirt, a
girl with curly hair and a striking facial resemblance to
Molly Tripp. Salter wondered for a second if some trick
was being played on him. It was an absurd idea;
nevertheless, he had the feeling that he was about to
watch Molly undress herself and shimmy, naked, and the
thought filled him with tension.

She started to dance, and almost immediately peeled
off her T-shirt. Fascinated, Salter nodded. That is how
she would look under her shirt. The music started again,
and the girl took off her jeans; she had thin, brown legs,

neither hairy nor deformed. Soon she kicked off her underwear and jigged happily around the little stage. As she came near them, Salter was sorry they had such a good table, because the following spotlight lit up O'Brien and him. He heard the music end with relief, but almost immediately it started again and the girl began a series of acrobatics designed to reveal her delicate and tender parts from all angles. Salter tried to look indifferent, but this made the girl mischievous, and she came to the edge of the stage and wiggled at him, her crotch only a yard from his face. He was appalled and he picked up his beer in defence, and the girl pouted at him, turned, and bent down to thrust herself in his face. Then she poked her hand through her thighs and stole his beer. The crowd cheered her wit, and after a bit of applause the spotlight finally went out.

The house lights went up to show O'Brien grinning at him. Salter looked around the club, and everyone else seemed to be grinning at him, too.

'You think you will recognize her again, Charlie?' O'Brien asked.

Salter realized, then, what was going on. 'You set that up, you bastard,' he said.

'It's a regular part of her act. You can order it for a friend, so tonight I asked them to honour you. Nice?'

Salter decided to tell his colleague of the extra dimension. 'If that happened to Summers, I can understand why he went home. That girl looked exactly like a student he thought he was in love with.'

O'Brien stopped grinning. 'It must have upset him. It looked as though it upset you.'

'Yes, and I hardly know the girl.'

After this the men walked back to Salter's hotel where they had a last quiet drink and reviewed their case.

'You don't think this Dunkley is likely?' O'Brien asked.

'On paper, yes. But not when you meet the man. He is

a good hater—almost enough motive in itself—and he must have got pretty jealous of Summers's lucky day. And he was already jealous of what he thought was going on between Marika Tils and Summers.'

'And you call this "on paper"? It would look pretty bad for Dunkley to someone who didn't have your feeling about him.'

'I know, and you'll probably have to prove he didn't do it, just to avoid arresting him for it. He's got a good alibi, though, along with Carrier. The one who knew Summers who doesn't have an alibi is Marika Tils, and I can't find anything phoney about her feeling for Summers.'

'So what do you think happened?'

'Either Summers was killed by an unknown stranger, or by an unknown (unknown to us, that is) friend.'

'Summers let them into his room, or they had another key. You don't think this Homer woman did it? *Her* story would look bad to a jury, too.'

'I know. No, I'm stuck with the whore theory, Onree. This must be your problem.'

'My instinct about the whores in this district is like yours for Summers's friends. I don't believe it, but I'll go through the motions. What we need to prove us both right, Charlie, is an unknown friend of Summers with all of Dunkley's motives and a taste for murder.'

'Right. Let's keep our eyes open.'

O'Brien offered to take the next day off and show Salter something of Montreal, but Salter declined, having a number of matters that required his attention in Toronto, including a squash lesson and a drink with Molly Tripp.

CHAPTER 7

In the years since Salter had courted Annie there, the Roof Bar had changed, but it was still the best bar in Toronto. The waiters still knew him, and watched now as Molly climbed on to the table. She took off her T-shirt and started to dance; then, as the waiters rushed to stop her she jumped up on to the stone balustrade that ran round the edge of the roof, and stepped out of her jeans, to pose for a second, naked. Salter jumped up after her, and she took his hand and stepped with him off the balustrade into space.

Salter awoke with a bump, sweating. Probably he had been shouting, too, but in a hotel bedroom in Montreal a little shouting is allowed. He showered and dressed quickly and took a cab to the station to eat his breakfast there while he waited for the train. He wanted badly to read a Toronto paper with his morning coffee to get back to normal.

In Toronto he phoned his wife and Sergeant Gatenby, and then, without calling ahead, took a cab to Jane Homer's office in Wollstonecraft Hall. The secretary tried to intercept him, but as she was announcing him he walked past her into the Dean's office. Jane Homer was calmer now. She still looked unhappy at seeing him but she no longer shook with misery, or fear. Salter came to the point quickly.

'When did you visit Professor Summers's room, Miss Homer?'

She protested, so he retreated a step and gave her the background of his question. 'We know that he put a key for you in your mailbox,' he said. 'At around two o'clock. We know that you got the key and wrote him a note—we have that note. We found the key in his room, and the desk-clerk remembers the rest. Now, when did you go to his room?'

'I went up there during the evening—about nine o'clock,' she said finally.

Salter waited.

'I know it sounds odd. But David left me his key so that I could let myself in and pour myself a drink while I waited, which I did. But he didn't come home early enough, so I went back to my room and to bed.'

'And that's that?'

'Yes.'

What a poor liar, Salter thought. What would this woman's motive for lying turn out to be? A good deal less than murder, he was certain.

'You have nothing else to tell me?'

She opened a desk drawer and took out a scrap of paper. 'This note was in the envelope with the key,' she said.

Salter read, 'If I'm not here when you get back, try later. I've had the most fantastic piece of luck.'

'Why didn't you show me this the other day?'

'Because I wanted to stay out of it. Because I was not involved in David's death and it would not help anything to know we were going to have a drink.'

'Did you? Have a drink? Just so that I know what else you don't think would help.'

'Yes. I poured myself one while I waited for him.'

'How long did you wait?'

'About half an hour.'

'What time, then, do you think you left the room?'

'About nine-thirty.'

'Anything else?'

'What do you mean?'

'I mean anything else, Miss Homer. *Anything else?*

'No. I went to David's room to have a drink. He did

turn up. That's all.'

'Did you often drink with Summers in hotel rooms?'

'That's enough, Inspector. I am just unlucky to be caught up in this. You know that.'

'I don't know anything, Miss Homer, except what I read in the papers and what people tell me. That's it, then?'

'There is nothing else. Now I have an appointment, please.'

Salter considered. He decided to keep what he had read to himself for the moment. 'All right, Miss Homer. Please don't go away, though, will you? I think we'll be in touch, shortly.'

She said nothing as he got up and left.

He walked back along College Street to his office where he was greeted by Gatenby with the news that the Superintendent wanted a report on the progress of the case by Monday. 'What case?' Salter grunted. 'What progress?'

He sat behind his desk and considered the note that Jane Homer had given him. It was bothering him, and he wanted to ask someone why. Then he isolated the phrase which troubled him, and phoned Mrs Summers.

'Inspector Salter here, Mrs Summers.'

'Hello. I wanted to thank you for coming by. I felt better after talking to you. Not terrific, but better. What can I do for you?'

'One of your husband's colleagues has remembered another phrase that he used on Friday when he was talking about his lucky day. He said your husband said he had had a "fantastic piece of luck". My question is simply: Would he have described the two thousand dollars he made in trading the Canadian dollar in those terms?'

'Your instincts are sound, Inspector. No, he wouldn't.

He didn't tell anyone much about his dealings, but, like I said, he made two or three thousand in a day several times. Lost it, too.'

'That's what I thought. Then what would he have called fantastic?'

'In money? A lot. Fifty thousand or more.'

'Could it be anything else?'

'Search me, Inspector. It sounds like money.'

'Have you had a chance to check his wallet? Maybe there is something there that we didn't notice?'

'I'll look for secret compartments, shall I? See, I'm joking already. No, I'll look, but I don't know what I'm looking for.'

'Nor do I. But the clue to your husband's behaviour that night was this stroke of luck, and if I can find out what it was we might be able to guess who he told, or who told him.'

'I'll look at it this afternoon.'

'Thank you, Mrs Summers.' Salter hung up the phone and stared at the note until it was time for his lesson.

They played for fifteen minutes without pause. Salter was splashing sweat on to the floor, but he was thrilled to note that his heart and lungs, while bursting, seemed to be getting used to the condition.

'Now,' said the pro. 'Let's have a little game. Best of five.'

They played a little game, the best of five points. 'Nice going,' called the pro, as Salter lumbered and dived after the ball. 'Terrific.' The pro won 3-2 and patted Salter with his racquet, one jock to another. 'Great stuff, chief,' he said. 'Tomorrow, same time?'

'Yes,' Salter wheezed. 'How do you think I'm doing? Could I play anyone around here, do you think?'

'Sure, Charlie. You could give Bill or Percy a game.'

Salter sat afterwards in the lounge, open-pored and

aching, watching the door. Bailey came through, on time, and Salter waved him over. He came to the table, somewhat reluctantly, Salter thought, and sat down:

'How about a game?' Salter asked.

Cranmer appeared, smiling like a shepherd. 'You could play on Monday, Bill,' he said. 'I have to cancel our game.'

Bailey looked irritated. 'Sure,' he said. 'Inspector . . .'

'Charlie,' corrected Salter.

'OK, Charlie, tomorrow, then. Four o'clock on the court?'

'Thanks, Bill.'

On Friday, after two days of doing nothing, except playing squash and waiting for O'Brien to call and say he'd found the killer, he met Molly, not on the Roof, but in a bar converted from a defunct gas station on Church Street where, thought Salter, instant food had replaced instant gas. He thought of an obvious joke but let it go as too obvious. 'Listen,' Molly said. He listened. Banjos and guitars and wailing voices. Country music. 'Ah!' he said. Salter did not have much music in his soul but this made his feet tap. 'What is it?' he asked.

' "The Lady's Choice Blue Grass Band!" Terrific, isn't it?'

'Nice,' he said cautiously. His night out in Montreal, followed by the nervous dream, had left him feeling disqualified from flirting with her, and he resolved that this would be the last time he would see her. He had thought about her, on and off, all day, and been unable to decide whether the dream represented desire, or fear, or what. Did he want to take her clothes off and grapple with her? What was he to her—Dad? He looked in the mirror behind the bar. One middle-aged policeman and one pretty (young) girl. When she looked in the mirror, what did she see?

It was time to go. She said, 'Let's go round the corner to Sam's. I want to buy a record.'

They finished their beer and walked through to Sam the Record Man on Yonge Street. 'Here,' she said, thumbing quickly through one of the country music racks. 'Here it is.' She pulled out a record of 'The Lady's Choice Blue Grass Band'. Salter reached for his wallet, but she pulled the record away from him and put a finger to her lips to indicate a secret. When she had paid and they were out on the street she turned to him and put the record in his hand. 'Happy Birthday,' she said.

'Christ, I forgot,' he said. It was one of the first things she had asked him.

She leaned up to him and kissed him beneath the ear and ran across Yonge Street, leaving him looking after her on the sidewalk.

At home there was a cake, a round of 'Happy Birthday to you', a new fountain-pen from his wife, and a set of jump cables from his sons. After dinner, Salter produced the record. 'Look,' he said, 'I heard this record today while I was having a cup of coffee, so I went and bought one. It was on a juke-box.'

Annie took the record and read the cover. The boys looked over her shoulder and broke into hysterics. Salter was mystified until Annie led him into the room containing the stereo where she pulled a record from a pile and showed him the cover. It was the same record.

'It's a Halifax group,' she said. 'My brother sent it to Angus for his birthday in March.'

'Have I ever heard it?'

'It's the one you are always yelling at Angus to turn down.'

'Is it?' Salter could think of nothing to say.

Annie said, 'Come upstairs.'

In the bedroom she asked, 'Who bought it for you? The

woman you were with this afternoon? The one you are having the affair with?'

'Yes,' he said. 'Yes, she did. But I am not having an affair.' And he told her the truth, or as much as he understood himself about Molly Tripp.

'Your father called,' Annie said on Sunday morning. They lay in bed after the most astonishing weekend in their marriage. The inevitable discussion of Molly Tripp had led to a much closer discussion of their own relationship which, though full of goodwill, had not been sharpened on the whetstone of a good talk for a long time. The result had been a miniature courtship, climaxing in a small honeymoon, so that they had spent most of the weekend making love with more enthusiasm than they had shown each other for years. The effect on Salter was a mild case of priapism. Even now, spent, and talking about his father, he lay rigid beside her.

'Not coming?' Salter asked, hopefully.

'Yes. He wants to bring a friend.'

'What!'

'A lady.'

'A girl-friend?'

'I imagine so. Maybe he's going to get married again.'

'For Christ's sake.' Salter withdrew into the bathroom. There he stood under a cold shower for several minutes before turning on the hot water to scrub himself. He felt purged, battered and clean. Annie came into the bathroom, and he put his arm up defensively.

'You playing squash this morning?' she asked.

'If I can,' he joked.

Annie ignored the facetiousness. 'Bring home some Brussels sprouts from one of the Chinese stores on Yonge Street. Your father is always asking for them.'

The pro played with his left hand, supplying the lesson

with a much-needed element of surprise. He still won
easily enough, but Salter got several points intentionally.
The weekend had made him feel lighter on his feet, and
he looked forward to meeting Bailey on the court.

His father arrived at six o'clock, accompanied by a stout
lady in her fifties dressed in a mushroom-coloured outfit
and wearing a hat like the Queen Mother's.

'This is May,' his father said, pointing at her as he did
so. He acted throughout the evening like May's owner,
drawing attention to her finer points when she was under
discussion, ignoring her when the conversation was
general. May said nothing whatever during dinner,
placidly eating Annie's roast beef, Brussels sprouts and
Lunenburg Pie like a large, well-trained child.

After dinner the boys disappeared, and Annie took
May for a walk so that the two men could chat in private.

His father said, 'I've been walking out with her for two
months now. She's Fred's widow. I expect you are
surprised.' He sat like a man in sudden possession of a
fortune, puffed-up and happy.

'I'm pleased, Dad. Annie is, too.'

'What about?'

'Well, that you've found a friend.'

'She's more than that.'

Salter blushed. As a child, he did not remember the
smallest reference to sex ever occurring in his parents'
house, and his father and he had kept up that
relationship. His father's remark sounded shockingly
bawdy.

'That's your privilege,' he said. Jesus Christ.

'We aren't going to get married,' his father said. Now
he was leering. 'We are going to live together.' He stared,
belligerent and proud, at his son, to see if he understood.

'Ah. Yes. Well, then. You won't be alone, will you?'

'It's not just for the company. I'm only sixty-seven. We

are having an affair.'

'Oh, well. That's all right then, isn't it?' Would the old (new) goat never shut up?

'It's more than all right. It's what my old man used to call "a bit of all right".' He leant forward and touched Salter's knee, and leered again. 'You know what I mean?'

Salter treated the question as rhetorical. 'Good for you, Dad,' he said loudly. 'Enjoy yourself while you can, eh?' Would you like some dirty magazines from the exhibits down at the station?

His father came to the second point. 'I've left everything to you, of course. Don't worry about that. We've both got good pensions.'

Salter was embarrassed. 'Spend it on yourself, Dad, and on May. Have a good time. We're all right.'

'I know that. I know *she's* got plenty.' His father always referred to Annie as 'she'. 'But I thought you might be expecting a bit from me.'

'Spend it, Dad. Spend it.' How much was involved? A thousand? Five?

'Right.' His father stood up and stroked his chest. 'We won't be having any çelebration. She's no blushing bride, after all, though she's made *me* blush a couple of times. The boys out, are they? Never do say cheerio properly, do they? Still. Here. Give them this.' He held out two ten-dollar bills.

'Nobody gives kids money when they visit any more, Dad.'

'I do. Here.'

Salter took the bills to avoid an argument and put them on the sideboard. Just then his wife returned with May, who was still silent but beaming and pink. His wife took charge, chattering appropriately. She kissed his father, who took her head in his hands and kissed her hard in return. Annie said, 'Isn't it great, Charlie? We're giving a party for them on July 5th.'

Salter wondered what had happened to the idea of no celebration, and he wondered, also, if his wife remembered that they were going to the Island on July 3rd. Before he could point out either of these objections, Annie said, 'I suggested it. So all you have to do is turn up.' This last remark was addressed to the happy couple.

In bed that night, Salter started to express his surprise, but she cut him off. 'Look at it selfishly,' she suggested. 'With luck, you have at least twenty years of it left.'

Salter stroked her back. 'Not at this rate,' he said, and curled, unmolested, around her.

Before he fell asleep, he asked, 'Is everybody doing it?'

'What?' she asked.

'I'll tell you tomorrow.'

Looking for Baghdad, he thought.

CHAPTER 8

On Monday morning Salter wrote up his report to date. Most policemen detest this aspect of their work, and Salter was like most policemen. An incompetent bank-robber may be caught in ten minutes, but it takes the rest of the day to write up a report on the incident suitable for Deputy Chiefs, Crown Attorneys, and the Supreme Court. In this case, however, he did not mind so much because he had nothing else to do that he could think of, and the sheer act of writing the report would enable him, force him, to review it systematically. He had been writing for two hours when he got a phone call from Mrs Summers. She had checked the wallet, and none of the lottery tickets were winners, although one would not be drawn until the following week. There was nothing else.

Except, 'There is one ticket missing, though,' she said.

'Missing? How do you know? Which one?'

'The local one. The weekly one. I was with him when he bought it the day before, so I know he had it. He must have checked it and thrown it away.'

'When was it drawn?'

'Thursday. The results are in the paper on Friday.'

'You are absolutely certain? And the ticket is not around the house?'

'Yes and no. I was with him, I told you. And he put the ticket in his wallet, like he always does.'

Now what? Salter felt as if he had won a lottery himself, but was too frightened to check the ticket carefully in case he was wrong. He tried to give himself breathing space by returning to the report, but he was unable to write a sentence. After a few minutes of indecision he phoned O'Brien in Montreal and told him of his conversation with Mrs Summers. Then he asked, 'Is there any way that the ticket could have been overlooked when the room was searched, Onree? The waste-basket, anything like that?' Salter's voice was plaintive.

'Wait, Charlie. Here is the man who looked after the scene. Speak to him.'

A detective with an accent much thicker than O'Brien's came on the line and Salter repeated his question.

'There was no ticket in the room, Inspector. You know those 'otel rooms. It was not an 'ard search. There was his clothes, the Scotch whisky, his suitcase, and the newspaper. And that's all. I checked the waste-basket myself. Not even a chewing-gum wrapper. Sorry, Inspector.'

'That's fine, Officer. Just fine. Thank you. Let me speak to Onree again. Thank you. Onree? Listen. I think I've got something. I think I've figured out what his lucky day was. I think he won a big lottery prize, and that he was killed for it, the ticket I mean. It's the only thing that was so big that he didn't want to tell anyone but couldn't keep it to himself, if you know what I mean. What do you think of that, Onree? Pure urcewl pworro.'

'Pure what, Charlie?'

'Pure urcewl pworro. You know. The guy in the stories.'

He heard O'Brien repeating the words to himself several times, then a shout of triumph, followed by some rapid French as O'Brien relayed something to his colleagues. Then, 'There are some flaws, Charlie.'

'I know that. It may all be bullshit, and it's certainly pure conjecture, but what do you think?'

'I think it's nice, Charlie. Let me think some more and we'll try to figure out how to prove it. I'll call you back this afternoon.'

Now. Salter found the number of the lottery organization and held his breath while he asked his first question. The answer was that no one had yet claimed the previous week's grand prize. The answer to the second was that the ticket had been bought in Mississauga. As far as he knew, there was no connection whatever between Summers and Mississauga. Shit.

Salter went to lunch.

Sergeant Gatenby poked his head round the door and addressed Salter who sat brooding after lunch. 'Visitors,' he announced in a stage whisper, gleefully.

Salter looked at him without interest. 'I'm busy,' he said. 'On a case.

'Oh, these *are* the case,' Gatenby said, rolling his eyes. 'A lady and a man. Miss Jane Homer and Professor Pollock.'

Now what could this mean? 'Show them in, Frank.'

Miss Homer entered first, pale and frightened. Behind her came Pollock, pipe in hand and boots ajar.

'Sit down,' Salter said, and waited.

Pollock began. 'I have been talking to Miss Homer, Inspector. I think she's been unwise and I've advised her to come and see you. She asked me to come with her.'

'Fine. Wait outside, please.'

'Miss Homer would prefer me to stay, I think.'

'Mr Pollock, I am conducting an inquiry into a brutal murder, not a student appeal. If Miss Homer wants to make a statement, I'll have it witnessed by my sergeant. If she wants a lawyer, I will phone for one. Are you a lawyer? No. Right. Wait outside.'

Pollock looked at the woman. 'I thought it might be like this,' he said. 'I'll wait outside. If you need your lawyer, I'll make sure he gets the message.'

Jane Homer said nothing, and Pollock left.

'Now, Miss Homer. You are going to tell me what fifth anniversary you were celebrating with Professor Summers, are you? I'll get Sergeant Gatenby.' Salter watched her start to shiver again and he went to the door to send the sergeant for a cup of tea. When Gatenby returned, he brought his notebook and a pencil.

Salter began. 'Miss Homer wants to make a statement. After she has finished, type it immediately and she will sign it. Go ahead, miss.'

She began in a tight, mechanical voice. 'When I arrived at the hotel in Montreal, there was a key waiting for me and a note from Professor Summers telling me to wait for him in his room.'

'We'll put the full note in the script, Miss Homer. I'll give it to the sergeant.'

She resumed. 'I went up to his room about nine, but there was no one there. So I left after half an hour.'

'Did you do anything while you were there?'

'I had a drink, and watched the television.'

'I see. And when did you come back?'

'At eleven-thirty.'

'To spend the night.'

'Yes.'

'To have intercourse with Professor Summers?'

'Yes.'

'He was expecting this?'

'Yes, we met every year.'

'At the conferences?'

'Yes.'

'You slept with Professor Summers once a year at the conferences?'

'Yes.'

'You never met him in Toronto?'

'No.'

A phrase occurred to Salter about the groves of academe.

'I see. Go on.'

'When I came back at eleven-thirty, I found David.'

'Dead?'

'Yes.'

'Would you describe the position of the body, and the state of the room, please?'

She did so, accurately.

'So. Why didn't you raise the alarm?'

'I am the Dean of Women at . . .'

'I know. You are the Dean of Women at Diddle-the-Girls Hall. So to avoid having your annual adultery exposed, you kept quiet about a murder.'

'Yes.'

'And then?'

'I left the next afternoon.'

'And that's that?'

'Yes. And now, I suppose, everyone will be involved.'

'Not necessarily. If what you say is true, it has nothing to do with my case and I won't involve you unnecessarily. It is possible you will be needed to substantiate the time of the death, which might be important, but I can't do anything about that. First, though, I have to decide whether I have the whole story from you.'

'You think I'm lying.'

'I don't think anything. I've had three separate stories

rom you so far, and I now don't believe or disbelieve
ny of them.'

'You think I killed David?'

'No, I don't, Miss Homer, but what I think is
rrelevant. It's my job to be suspicious, especially where I
ave cause.'

'Are you going to arrest me?'

'Not unless this story turns out to be phoney, too. Will
t?'

'Of course not.'

'Then, no. But, once more, Miss Homer: Do you have
anything more to tell me?'

'No. I have nothing to do with any of this. I think like
everyone else that poor David was probably killed by a
prostitute or her associate.'

'If he was waiting for you, that's hardly likely, is it?'
Salter asked, though he wondered himself. Who could say
what the effect of seeing Molly dancing naked on the
able was on the slightly infatuated professor of romantic
poetry?

'May I go now?'

'Would you wait in this office, please, while the
statement is being typed.' Salter led her into a little side
office, like a cupboard. Gatenby looked up from his
notebook when the door had closed. 'These academic
conferences,' he said. 'Just a sea of heaving arses, you
might say, eh, Inspector?'

Salter grunted at him. 'Type the report, Frank, and tell
Pollock to come in here.'

Pollock came in and sat down. 'May I smoke,
Inspector?' he asked, indicating the pipe and his tobacco
pouch.

'No. You know what Miss Homer told me?'

'Yes. I told her to come and make a clean breast of it.
The smell bother you, does it?'

'Should I believe her?'

'Oh yes.' Pollock still had not put his smoking materials away.

'Oh yes? Why?'

'Because I know who killed David,' Pollock said, and now with the air of a man who had earned the right, he began to fill his pipe.

Salter watched him for a few seconds, a long time, feeling all the professional frustrations and the private emotional turbulence of the last few days pile up, and he went mad.

'Professor,' he shouted, making the title sound like a term of abuse, 'if you know anything about Summers's death you have an obligation to the law to reveal it. If you've just been doing a little theorizing in your office, then forget it. What I do need, if you have any, is information. Now. You've got something to say? *And don't light that bloody pipe!*'

Pollock weathered this fairly well. 'No,' he said. 'I haven't. But Professor Carrier has. He should be here now. May I see?' Without waiting for a response he opened the door to the outside office. 'There we are. Come on in, Paul.'

Carrier came in, looking distraught. He allowed Pollock to lead him to the chair and sat down. Pollock placed his boots at right-angles and stood at his shoulder, sucking his unlit pipe.

'Go ahead, Paul,' Pollock said.

Carrier looked up at Pollock, who nodded and pointed with his pipe at the inspector. Carrier began, 'Dunkley wasn't in my room on Thursday night when David was killed. He must have done it.'

'Hold on, please. I gather you are now changing your story, Professor. Let's have it again. When wasn't Dunkley in your room?'

'Between ten o'clock and twelve o'clock.'

'Why did you tell me he was?'

'He asked me to. He swore he had nothing to do with David's death, but he was honour bound not to tell me where he was.'

'Oh, great. And you swore, on your professor's honour, not to let him down, did you? But now you think he might have killed your friend. Before, you didn't think so. Now you do. I see. This is wonderful. What made you change your mind?'

Pollock said, 'I did, Inspector. He confided in me and I told him to come and see you.'

'You did, did you, Professor? When?'

'He told me about it right away, last weekend. But I only advised him to see you today.'

'I see. Just before I charge both of you with making false statements and withholding evidence, do you mind telling me why?'

'Jane Homer confided in me yesterday. She said you had interviewed her twice. I thought you might suspect her, so I thought it was time you got the whole of Paul's story.'

'Now let me see. You didn't think Dunkley could have done it until you thought I was accusing Miss Homer. Then you thought he might have. What a detached witness you make. That the academic mind at work, Professor? The literary mind?'

'I was about to tell you, anyway, Inspector, or advise Paul to. I changed my mind because Dunkley is obviously cracking up!'

'Is he? Why is that? You know why, of course?'

'What else could it be?'

'Perhaps he's terminally ill. Perhaps his cat has died. I could give you a thousand reasons. All right, Mr Pollock. Let me tell you what you are going to do. I haven't made up my mind how much to charge you with yet, but in the meantime you are going to go back to your study and stay there, keeping your mind open and your mouth shut.

Don't speculate about this case with anyone, unless the killer asks your advice in which case discuss it with me. Now get out, please. As for you, Mr Carrier, I'll get a statement from you and ask you to wait, too, while it is being typed. I may hold you for further questioning. You realize, of course, that if Dunkley has no alibi, then neither have you.'

Pollock said, 'Oh, that's ridiculous, Inspector.'

'Shut your goddamn face, you. Get out,' Salter screamed. 'Go on. Out!'

Pollock, shaken finally, moved to the door. 'I think you are making an error, Inspector,' he offered.

'Frank,' bawled Salter. The sergeant put his head round the door. 'Frank, I want Professor Pollock charged with withholding evidence. He can have bail. Back here at ten in the morning.' Salter dismissed Pollock and turned to Carrier. 'Now. Your statement, please, Professor.'

Pollock was led out looking dazed, still sucking his pipe.

While he was waiting for Carrier's statement to be typed, Salter phoned Montreal. He was connected with O'Brien immediately.

'Onree,' he said, 'a few developments. First, it looks as if you can forget about the whore theory. I found out whose lipstick that was on the glass.'

'Jane Homer's?'

'Right, but I believe she had nothing to do with this.'

'She was in the room, Charlie.'

'They were lovers, but she never saw him that night until he was dead. She let herself in at eleven-thirty and found him dead.'

'You believe this, Charlie?'

'Yes, I do. They used to meet once a year. I read about it in his diary. This was their fifth anniversary. Somebody wrote a play about this kind of thing. It happens all the time, apparently. It's a cliché.'

'Romantic. Anything else?'

'Yes,' Salter said reluctantly. 'Two of the people he had dinner with have no alibis for the time Summers was killed. One of them was his worst enemy.'

'Ah?'

'Ah nothing, Onree. Tell you the truth, I think this is what these people would call a sub-plot, but Christ knows how it will tie in.'

'But you will question this . . . ?'

'Dunkley. Oh, sure. It's all a bit phoney, though. He hated Summers and Summers disliked him.'

'So therefore he didn't kill him? This is Anglo police thinking?'

'No, no, don't start calling me a Wasp, Onree. But everyone, including people who don't like Dunkley, has said he couldn't possibly have killed Summers. His wife, even. And Jane Homer.'

'But you *will* pick him up?'

Salter sighed. 'Yes, tomorrow. I'll call you.' He hung up, and dialled the number of the chairman of the English Department.

'Professor Browne? Salter here. No, we don't have a 'Yard' in Toronto, Professor. I want you to do me a favour. First, do you know where Mr Dunkley is?'

'Yes, he's right here in the office.'

'Oh shit.'

'No, no, Inspector. *Nil desperandum.* I meant only "at work" rather than "at home". He's in his own office. He can't hear us.'

'Good. Would you make an appointment with him to see you at ten in the morning? I want to make sure that he stays in town, but I am afraid that if he knows that I want to see him he may disappear.'

'Really, Inspector? Blood on his hands?'

'Don't be silly. I think he might just not want to talk to

me. And, Professor. Please. Not a word to anyone.'

'Mum's the word. I'll think of some excuse.'

Salter hung up and called out to his sergeant, 'I'm going downtown, Frank, on some errands. I'll see you in the morning.'

But Gatenby had seen Salter's appointment book. 'Have a good game, boss,' he called back cheekily.

Salter was going to lose, there was no doubt about that. Bailey was not very good, but the policeman had not been playing long enough to get to his level. Nevertheless, he was giving him a game. The first one he lost 9-0, the second, 9-3, and the third, 9-1. End of set. Now Salter was serving to open the second set. He served, and Bailey smashed the ball into the corner, too low. Salter served again, and the ball dropped dead in the back corner, giving Bailey no chance. 2-0 to Salter. He served again and Bailey made a good return, curling the ball along the left side wall for a certain winner. Salter dug at the ball, two-handed, like an idiot playing golf, and managed to scrape it back along the wall, catching Bailey off-balance. Bailey stared at the ball for a moment, then said, 'Shovelling is illegal.'

Salter said, 'Your point, then?'

'No, no. Just mentioning it, see. In a needle match you wouldn't be able to do that.'

'Let's play it like that, then.'

'No. no. That's fine. Go ahead. I was just pointing it out.'

Salter prepared to serve. He had no sense of having 'shovelled' the ball. There had been a hitting sound when he connected, soft but clear. He served again. Bailey returned the ball carefully, and Salter rushed at it. He connected with the handle of his racquet and the ball dropped soggily off the front wall. Bailey threw himself at it and got it on the second bounce. Salter let the shot go past him, and bent to pick the ball up. Bailey put out his hand for it.

Salter said, 'I thought it bounced twice.'

'No, no,' Bailey said. 'I got it.' He took the ball and got ready to serve.

Now Salter knew what he was up against. During the first set Bailey had roared around the set like a man chasing chickens. He slowed down when he was well ahead in the second set, offering Salter a few tips until Salter won two points in a row, then he started roaring and smashing again. In the third set Salter had tried only to defend himself as Bailey raged about him. The level of body contact increased, and twice Bailey hit him with the ball, as it seemed to Salter, intentionally. This was the first time he had actually cheated, though. Salter decided to have a go.

Bailey served, Salter returned it and Bailey banged it back. Salter tipped it gently against the front wall as he had seen Cranmer do, and crouched out of the way. Bailey hit him in the ankle with his racquet, and shouted, 'Let.'

'What?'

'You were in the way of my shot,' Bailey said. 'We play the point again.' He served again. This time Salter tipped it immediately against the front wall and jumped clear of any possible 'let'. Bailey dived for the ball and crunched himself against the wall. He got up and shook himself. 'I can't stand that soft shit,' he said. 'Summers used to do it. It fucks up the game.'

It's legal, though, thought Salter, and served. Bailey smashed it, below the line. 4-0 to Salter. Salter served again, and this time Bailey tried a soft shot against the front wall, and missed. 5-0. Salter had not enjoyed himself so much for years. He served again, but Bailey now hit a perfect return which Salter missed. Bailey served, very aggressively, and ran to the centre of the court ahead of Salter's return. The ball hit him in the back. 'Jesus Christ you've got the whole fucking court,' he shouted.''But you were standing where I wanted to hit it,' Salter said mildly. He served again and Bailey smashed it home for a winner. Now Bailey served carefully, and by playing warily won the next five points without any difficulty. 5-5. The lights went out at that point and the two men walked off the court, dripping.

Over the beer, which Salter insisted on signing for, Bailey recovered himself as Salter asked him to explain what was legal, what was 'fair', and what was unsporting. Bailey explained, rising to the bait of Salter's mock humility. 'That soft stuff is "legal",' he said, 'but it ruins the game. In my opinion, anyway. Old Dave used to do it a lot. You noticed when we started playing properly how the game got better.'

'Is that how he won the last game you played?'

Bailey looked confused. 'Well, yes,' he said, after a few seconds. 'He couldn't beat me in the open court. But he could work that soft shit real well.'

They were interrupted by the waitress with the charge for Salter to sign.

'Want another, Inspector?' Bailey asked.

'Sure. Tomorrow?'

'I meant a beer. But OK. Same time, then.'

Cranmer appeared at their table. 'Beating Metro's finest, Bill?' he asked, nodding at the slip the waitress was returning to Salter. And then, 'Any news, Inspector?'

Salter shook his head. 'Lots of suspects, but no clues, Percy. We are continuing our inquiries.'

No one wanted to pursue the subject, and the two players rose to go to the showers. 'After you, Charlie,' Bailey said, with a flourish of courtesy.

The next morning Salter waited in the chairman's office. It was five to ten and they were expecting Dunkley. 'You want me to become invisible when he arrives?' Browne asked.

'If I could use your office, it would probably be best.'

'I shall be in the library if you want me. Ah! Come in, Stewart, come in. I'm afraid I've deceived you. It is the Inspector who wants to talk to you.' Browne smiled falsely, and slid his bulk through the door, closing it scrupulously after him.

Salter pointed to a chair, but Dunkley remained standing. 'I presume this is still in regard to Summers's death?' he asked.

'Unless you've anything else on your conscience, Professor?'

Dunkley folded his arms and said nothing.

'Sit down,' Salter said sharply.

Dunkley sat down then, and refolded his arms.

'Now. I'd like to know where you were between ten o'clock and twelve o'clock on the night Summers was killed.'

'I see I have been betrayed. I have nothing to say.'

'In that case you can get your hat and say nothing down at the station.'

'I'm ready to go now.'

Salter stood up. 'Let's go, then.'

Dunkley preceded him, still with his arms folded, out to the corridor where they found Marika Tils and Paul Carrier in close and agitated conversation. Shit, thought, Salter, I forgot to remind that fat chairman to keep his mouth shut. Carrier looked white, and Marika Tils clutched at Dunkley as he went by, but Dunkley shook her off and marched down the hall to the elevator. The two men left the building and drove to the station.

'Now,' Salter said, when they were in his office. 'You are entitled to have a lawyer present, and to stay silent if you want, because you are under suspicion, but I'm not charging you with anything yet. I simply want the true story.'

Dunkley looked out of the window and crossed his legs, locking himself up tight.

'For Christ's sake,' said Salter, 'You are a well-known enemy of Summers, you were in Montreal, and you refuse to say where you were when he was killed. What do you expect me to do?'

Dunkley stared out of the window.

Salter tried again. 'If you won't speak, I shall have to send a squad to your residence to look for evidence— blood, whatever— and if it's there, they'll find it.'

Dunkley spoke now. 'You won't find anything,' he said. 'I didn't kill Summers.'

'Then would you mind telling me *why* you won't say where you were?'

'I was not alone. That's all. It's a matter of loyalty. I told Carrier that, and he gave me his word.'

'Oh, fuck this,' Salter said exasperated. 'Sergeant! I want the boys to go to this man's house and look for the usual. Hold him here for obstructing the police.'

Dunkley broke his pose. 'I'm under arrest?'

'Of course you are under arrest. What do you think? Frankly, Professor Dunkley, I'm just covering my ass. I may be wrong, but I don't think you've the guts to kill a mouse. I think you are on some kind of trip, right now, and I'm too busy to find out what it is. When I have a moment, I'll question you further, just because I'm curious about what you are up to.'

'In the back room? Where no one can see, or hear?'

'No. I think you might enjoy that. No, right here. I may invite a few friends, though. Now sit there and don't resist arrest. My sergeant is liable to give you a nasty pinch if you try to run away.'

For something had been bothering Salter all night. He

borrowed an empty office and sat down with a pad of paper to go through the exercise of writing the report once more. After half an hour of laborious detail, he stopped and went back to the first page. He read the list of items that had been found in the room, again and again. Then, he read the account of the discovery of the body and got his first solid confirmation that he wasn't going off half-cocked. He phoned O'Brien, who was out, but then he was put through to the detective who first went into Summers's room.

'There was a *Globe and Mail* in the room,' he said. 'What state was it in?'

'There was some blood on it.'

'No, Officer. I mean, had it been read?'

'It was open, yes.'

'What section? The *Globe* is in three or four sections.'

'The front section. The first page inside.'

'And the other sections—Business, Sports?'

'You can see in the picture. They 'adn't been touched.'

'Thank you, Officer. Tell Sergeant O'Brien I called, will you? And tell him I still think I'm right.'

In a fever he dialled Mrs Summers's number. When she replied, he asked, 'You say you drove your husband to the station on Friday morning. Was he very late?'

'He had to run like hell, Inspector. I was surprised that he made it.'

'He didn't stop to buy a paper?'

'No, I told you. He was *late*.'

'Sorry, Mrs Summers. Now did he get a chance to read the paper at home?'

'We don't get it delivered. I stopped it when he got interested in commodities, because he spent the first hour of the day adding up his winnings, or his losses. It drove me mad.'

'Thank you, Mrs Summers.'

One more check, the broker. 'Leslie Stone? Inspector

Salter here. I want to ask you a question you've already answered, but I want to be sure of it. When you told Professor Summers about his profit on the Canadian dollar, was that news to him?'

'Absolutely, sherriff. He cheered and said something about the gods were smiling on him, this really *was* his lucky day.'

'What do you think he meant?'

'It sounded to me like he'd heard all kinds of good news that day.'

'That's what I think too, Miss Stone. Thanks.'

'You're welcome.'

Now. Which one of them had Summers told about his ticket? The fact that the ticket had been bought in Mississauga, a fact which might make nonsense of his hunch, would clear itself up, he felt certain. Mississauga lay just outside Toronto along the Lakeshore, towards Oakville. Lots of people lived there and worked in Toronto, and the other way round.

He sat there wondering what to do next. He was utterly certain now of why Summers had been murdered; he was also certain he knew who had done it if only his brain would disgorge the information. He phoned O'Brien again in Montreal and found him in. After some pleasantries, Salter said, 'I'm sure of it, Onree. Summers bought a lottery ticket, he was checking the results on page two of the *Globe* on Friday afternoon in his hotel room; he told everybody after that that that was his lucky day. Whoever killed Summers has the lottery ticket. There's only one flaw: the winning ticket was bought in Mississauga, and there's no way Summers could have bought it. Even if he did, the one he bought, that his wife saw him buy, is missing.'

There was a long silence. Then O'Brien said, 'Charlie, you must be right, but there's something missing. You will have to wait to see who cashes the big winning ticket.'

His voice was comforting.

'Yeah, right. And if it is a little old lady in Mississauga, I'll clap her in jail on a charge of having been in Montreal that night, having heard about Summers's win, having beaten him over the head, and having snuck back to Mississauga without anyone noticing.'

'Do you have any other suspects, Charlie?'

'I'm holding Dunkley, and there is one other left, a quiet little guy, colleague of Summers, who looks harmless, but I'm learning a lot about absent-minded professors who aren't what they seem.'

'My advice is to give it a rest for a while, Hercules. Let your grey cells go to work on it.'

'How do I arrange that, Onree?'

'Go to the races.'

Salter hung up and sat with his cobweb theory dissolving in his hands but unable to get clear of it. He could see nothing to do. He sat at his desk, doing nothing, until it was time for his game with Bailey which, he reflected, as he stood up to go to the squash club, might qualify for O'Brien's approval as a sufficiently absorbing activity to release his mind to get on with its work unconsciously, without interference from its owner.

Bailey won again, but this time Salter nearly won a set. Bailey said, 'You're getting pretty good, Charlie. I can't let down at all.'

Next time, buddy, Salter thought.

'Beer?' he asked.

'Sure. It's costing you a few beers, learning this game.' Bailey was trying to be a good winner, but it was hard.

The two men drank their beer, while Salter listened to some helpful tips from his opponent and master. What was even worse was when Bailey, in a burst of expansiveness, and contrary to all the agreed etiquette, tried to pay for the beer. Salter grabbed the charge slip from the girl's hand and said, 'Loser pays.'

'OK, OK,' Bailey said. 'But it could be expensive.'

Salter drank his beer quickly, trying to look agreeable. Christ, he thought, it's just a game. I'm getting as bad as Summers. He left the club and walked over to the subway station, thinking of Summers, and Dunkley, and lottery tickets, and Mississauga, and getting nowhere. He seriously thought of phoning Molly Tripp, but he rejected it, because he could not think of an excuse, and because he did not want to show himself to her in a sour mood. Besides, Annie would probably guess.

He went home, ate his dinner, still brooding, snarled at the kids for watching television day in, day out, turned his back on the tentative advances of Annie in bed, and woke up depressed, just like the old days.

CHAPTER 9

At the office he phoned O'Brien, his only friend, for a chat, but the Frenchman was out, of course. The Oldest Sergeant in the Force brought him some coffee and reminded him that Dunkley was still in the cells.

Salter said, 'He didn't do it, Frank. I'm right back where I started. Whoever killed Summers did it for a bloody winning lottery ticket, or something like that'—his confidence in his theory was ebbing—'and someone knew what Summers's lucky day was.'

'Why don't you try that end?' Gatenby said. 'Ask them again, straight out, if they have any idea of what Summers's lucky day was.'

What an asshole, thought Salter, automatically. Still, it was something to do. He started by phoning Usher. He worked out a twist on the question.

'Mr Usher,' he asked, 'do you remember if anyone was

alone at any time on the Friday night, and was anyone, apart from Summers, acting strangely? I mean, at any time were all of you in the washroom except Summers and one person? Anything like that?'

But Usher was unable to remember anything. Nor could Marika Tils or Carrier.

Salter gave up. 'Frank,' he called. 'Bring Dunkley in here.'

When the professor was led in, slightly unkempt after his night in the cells, Salter tried to be brisk and cunning.

'Mr Dunkley. Before I proceed with the rest of the charges I'd like to clear up one or two details. We know now that you had the motive and the opportunity to kill Summers. What was the straw that broke the camel's back? Was it Summers's piece of luck you couldn't stand the idea of? When did he confide in you, by the way? In the bar?'

Dunkley looked at him in contempt. 'What a pathetic flounderer you are, Inspector. Is this typical?'

Salter looked back at Dunkley, wondering whether to bother charging him with anything, for he was as certain as ever that he was the wrong man. They were interrupted by a commotion in the outer office. A constable put his head round the door to say that a Professor Pollock was causing a disturbance.

'Bring him in here,' Salter said.

When Pollock was led in he immediately ran at Dunkley, knocking him out of his chair. They rolled together on the floor as Pollock tried to punch his colleague.

'You dirty, rotten bastard,' screamed Pollock. 'You slimy, filthy, rotten pig.' And much more besides.

Salter picked the two men apart and held Pollock, spitting and cursing, while Dunkley stood back against the wall, straightening his clothes. When Pollock stopped shouting, Salter relaxed his hold, and the professor launched himself across the room and tried to hit Dunkley again, who crouched without making any effort to defend himself. Salter hauled Pollock away again and dragged him out of the office, handing him over to a constable to 'lock up until he cools off'.

When he returned to his own office, Dunkley was seated again. 'What was that all about?' Salter asked.

'I have no idea,' Dunkley replied, trying to recover his former pose.

'Oh, for Christ's sake! Frank!' The sergeant poked his head round the door, grinning in glee. 'Take this idiot back to the cells, will you? I'll tell you when to do anything about him.'

Gatenby said, 'There's a lady to see you, Chief.' He rolled his eyes to indicate that Dunkley should not know who it was.

'All right. Take his learned gentleman away and bring her in.'

Marika Tils entered, looking frightened.

'Churchey la fucking femme,' Salter said.

'What?'

'It's French. It means I should have known it would be you.'

'You were right, then. Has Professor Pollock been to see you?'

'Yes. Professors Dunkley and Pollock met in my office and tried to have a fight. Or rather, Pollock did. The trouble was that he has forgotten how, if he ever knew, so he didn't hurt Dunkley much. Hitting people is harder than it looks on TV.'

'They were fighting over me.'

'Fighting over your favours, were they?'

'Yes.'

'I was joking. They really were?'

'Yes. Toby had found out that Dunkley had made love to me.'

'In Montreal, of course, on Friday night. Who is Toby?'

'Toby Pollock. Yes, in Montreal.'

'My sergeant was right. These conferences of yours sound like giant games of musical beds.'

'I didn't want to sleep with Dunkley.'

'Tell me the whole story. Who did what, where, why, and most of all, when.' Salter was sick of this gang. His head was buzzing with an idea that had nothing to do with this nonsense, but he had to complete this part of the investigation in case his latest idea was insane.

She began. 'Dunkley has always been jealous of David and me.'

'Not Pollock, your lover, but Summers?'

'Yes. I told you, he knows nothing of Toby and me.'

'He does now. Go on.'

'I told you, David Summers and I were friends, not lovers. But Dunkley thought we were. Lovers, I mean. He saw us always together, and he assumed. He was jealous because he wanted me, but I didn't like him. Several times when there had been drinking, at a party or something, he got me in a corner and asked me to go to bed with him. But I told him and I told him, and I thought finally he had given in because he—what, lay off?'

'Laid off.'

'Yes. It doesn't feel right, grammatically. Anyway, he laid off me. Until Montreal. Then someone told him a bit of gossip about David's annual rendezvous with a lady at the conference.'

'You knew about that?'

'We all did. David confided in everybody about it. But he never said who it was. When David bought us all dinner, and told us about his lucky day, and went home early after *I* went home early, Dunkley put it all together and decided I was David's annual event, his lucky day, so to speak. When he and the others came back to the hotel,

he waited for a little while and phoned David's room.
There was no answer, because, I suppose, David was
already dead. But he decided David was in my room. So
he came to my room and banged on the door. I didn't
answer at first, but he kept on banging so I told him to go
away through the door. But he was shouting that he knew
I had David in there and he wouldn't go away, so I
opened the door to show him. Then he was sorry and told
me how much he loved me and asked me to let him stay
with me. This went on and on and on. In the end I
thought maybe he would go away if he got what he
wanted so I asked him and he said he would, so that's
what I did.'

'You let him make love to you, to get rid of him?'

'I was exhausted, Inspector. Besides, it's no big deal.'

'It was for Dunkley.'

'Oh yes. Afterwards he thanked me. I got rid of him
then and that was the end of it, I thought, until today,
when I realized I was his only alibi and he would never use
me because he is a man of honour.' She spoke without
passion; she was evidently worn out.

'So you decided to come and see me.'

'No, I was idiotic. I told Toby. He went crazy.' She
slumped in her chair. 'What a lot of fuss over a little
fuck.'

'I'll sort these two out, Miss Tils. Go home and take the
phone off the hook. One last question. Are you sure of the
time when Dunkley was in your room?'

'Certain. At eleven he was banging on my door. At ten
past eleven he was in my room. At twelve he was in my
bed. I had the TV on. The news, the weather, and "O
Canada".'

In spite of his irritation, Salter laughed. 'You should
have told me all this days ago, Miss Tils. As you say, we
have all been put to a great deal of trouble over one little
fuck.'

She made a face and stood up. 'You know what pisses me off, Inspector? The three of us won't be able to live in the department after this, so one of us will have to go. Dunkley should go; if not him, then Toby. But I will go. They have tenure, and I'm just a woman they are fighting over. And my appointment is for one year only.' She shouldered her bag, and left.

Salter called in the sergeant. 'Frank,' he said, 'I want you to hold those guys for the rest of the day. Let them go, one at a time, at the end of the day shift, and warn them that if either one speaks to Marika Tils or tries to speak to the other one before I give my permission, it will be a criminal offence.'

'It won't, will it, chief?' Gatenby said, in the voice of a doubting yokel.

'Of course not, you silly sod. But it might keep them apart for a few hours if they think so. Let Dunkley go first; tell the patrol to drive him to his house and sit outside for half an hour. Then come back and take Pollock home; same routine. Then have them park outside Marika Tils's place until I give the word.'

'Right, chief. I'll give her full power when we go over the reef,' said Gatenby, leaving Salter to wonder if he was being made fun of.

When Gatenby returned, Salter was still staring out of the window.

'No good, chief?'

'No good, Frank. Dunkley didn't know. No one knew.'

'Someone must have,' Gatenby said.

In a minute, thought Salter, he's going to ask me if I've looked in all my pockets, just like my mother did when I'd lost something.

Gatenby said, 'Perhaps he told someone else?'

Very rarely, his mother would keep on until she suggested a place he had not thought of, the right place. 'Did you leave it in your raincoat?' she would say. 'You went to school with it on, but you didn't bring it home.'

Salter stared at Gatenby for a very long time. Then, 'Frank,' he said, 'you are a fucking genius.'

'I was only trying to help,' Gatenby said. 'There is no need to be sarcastic.'

'I wasn't being sarcastic, Frank. You are a fucking genius. Now leave me alone.'

He went over the details for an hour. It had to be right even if there was still a piece missing. Eventually he made two phone calls, one to O'Brien and one to the squash club.

O'Brien said, 'You'll have to be careful, Charlie. If he knows what you are up to, you won't find a thing. You may not find anything anyway, if he's destroyed it.'

'I'll find *something*, Onree. He can't cover up a trip like that.'

'If he did it.'

'I *know* he did it.'

'Jump him, Charlie. Frighten him.'

'OK. Onree, I'll call you.'

'Good luck.'

Salter had the afternoon to wait until he could go down to the squash club. He went for a walk along College Street to Parliament Street, then for a long ramble through Cabbagetown, in the area where he had grown up when they still grew cabbages in the front yard. When he had used up enough time he headed for the squash club to intercept Bailey. First he phoned Gatenby.

'Frank,' he said, as soon as the sergent answered, 'send a car to this address.' He gave the location of Bailey's apartment. 'I want the place turned over. I'll get a warrant tomorrow.' He told the sergeant what he was looking for.

'Right you are, boss,' Gatenby said. 'Just like the old days, isn't it? For you, I mean. I was always on traffic duty, myself.'

'Move, for Christ's sake, Frank. I should have done this an hour ago.'

He went back and stationed himself in the lounge by the door. At a few minutes to four, Bailey came in, and Salter hailed him.

'Could I have a word, Bill? Won't take a minute.'

Bailey sat down. 'I have a game with Percy at four,' he said.

Maybe, thought Salter, and took a deep breath. 'Bill,' he said, 'if Summers won his last game with you, why did he pay for the beer?'

Bailey went grey, and Salter should have stopped there, but he was unable to. He continued: 'And when he phoned you from Montreal, did he tell you how much he'd won on the lottery?'

It was a hit all right, but Bailey had now had the few seconds necessary to start him talking. 'He didn't win any lottery,' he said. 'Not that I know of.'

Salter tried a lie. 'He told his broker he'd won a fortune on a lottery. He phoned you right after. Didn't he say anything about it?'

Cranmer arrived, and Bailey stood up. 'No. Not a word. Jesus, poor guy. That it, then?'

'That's it, Bill,' Salter said, and the two players disappeared into the changing-room.

Have I fucked it up, thought Salter, as he waited for the call from Bailey's apartment? Am I wrong?

After five minutes, Cranmer emerged from the changing-room in squash costume. 'Seen Bill anywhere?' he asked Salter. 'He's disappeared and we start at four-ten.'

Salter made a dive for the phone. 'The man is on his way,' he said when he got through. 'Hold him at the apartment. Any excuse. I'll be there in five minutes. He ran down the back stairs of the club, and within a few seconds was able to commandeer a passing cruiser. On the way to Bailey's apartment, he raised Gatenby on the radio.

'News?' the sergeant said. 'I'll say. Your man saw our car outside his apartment and took off. Luther is following him in the squad car. They are travelling along the Lakeshore. Luther wants to know how hard to go for him if there is a real chase.'

'Tell Luther he's wanted for murder. Don't lose him.' The light gleamed within the cave; with a quarter of a mile to go, Salter's horse emerged smoothly from the pack, bearing down on the finish line.

'What's the word from the search?' he asked.

'Nothing yet.'

'Tell him to stay there. I'm on my way over.'

It took another ten minutes to get to Bailey's apartment; they travelled with all the noise and lights the car could supply. Inside the apartment, a detective was sitting down, smoking. He said, 'Phase one is over, boss. No obvious places left. The next stage takes a long time. You want it done?'

'Not yet. Maybe. We might not need it.' Salter looked around. 'He's running, and that's just as good.' He walked around the apartment, glancing at all the drawers the searchers had left open, and picked up a small iron key attached to an elastic wrist-band, which was lying on the kitchen counter.

'Where did you find this?'

'In his laundry basket. We figured it had dropped out of his tennis shorts.'

'Squash,' Salter said absently.

'Is it important?'

'It might be.'

The driver of the commandeered squad car appeared at the door. 'Message for you, sir. The guy they were chasing ran off the road trying to make the turn on to the 417. They are waiting for the ambulance.'

'Take me back to the squash club,' Salter said. He turned to the detective. 'Tidy up here, and wait for me. Don't look for anything else yet.'

In the car, he said, 'You can switch the noise gear off.' Nevertheless, when they got to the club he ran up the steps to the changing-room where the row of little wooden lockers was situated. The key opened No. 23, and Salter peered, frightened, into the cave. Inside were two lottery tickets.

'What put you on to it?' the Superintendent asked.

'The charge slip for the beer at the squash club,' Salter said. 'Right from the beginning I knew that Summers had won the Wednesday night game, but he paid for the beer. Why? Either he was being generous, which would have pissed Bailey off mightily, or the bet was something else. When I got on to the missing lottery ticket, I realized what had happened. They bet their lottery tickets—no big deal at a dollar each—but Bailey's won, and Summers couldn't resist phoning him from Montreal and crowing. Bailey went crazy—not about the money so much as the way he had lost it, and to Summers. So he flew down to Montreal and waited for Summers to come back from his night out.'

'Then he just beat his head in to get the ticket?'

'Not quite. He says he just wanted to get half the winnings, or get the ticket from Summers and throw it away so that neither of them could have it. But Summers wasn't as drunk as he seemed, and he caught Bailey going through his wallet after Bailey thought that Summers had passed out. Bailey knew he was finished then, so, in a panic, he killed Summers, and ran. Afterwards, when he realized he might get away with it—Summers had told him he was waiting for someone else—he kept the ticket, thinking to 'find' it in his wallet in a month's time. After all, no one else knew about it, and who would connect it with Summers?'

'This is very cute figuring, Salter. Put it all in your report. Tell me, why didn't you follow up this charge slip when you first saw it?'

'I didn't realize the significance of it, sir.'

'Don't put that in the report, then. Put, "When I rechecked the contents of the wallet, I saw that one of the charge slips was for a bill that the accused should have paid." '

'Right, sir.'

'Now. When you found out that the winning ticket was bought in Mississauga, why didn't you check the addresses of all suspects? Then you would have found out that Bailey's company has a factory there.'

'I thought my theory was wrong, sir. I didn't realize that someone was trying to get his own ticket back.'

'Don't put that. Put, "I decided, then, to check on the Mississauga connections of all suspects." Then what did you do?'

'I went to the squash club to talk to Bailey. But before I could question him properly he left.'

'Jesus Christ. You asked him if he did it? Right there in the squash club?'

'More or less, yes, sir.'

'For Christ's sake. Put, "I began by checking up on Bailey, who was then at the squash club. However, something in my manner must have put him on his guard, for he left the club quickly. I called for help to search his apartment and arrest him if necessary." A lot of this is still guesswork, Salter. Can you prove enough of it?'

'The guesswork is concerned with his motive, sir. We've found traces of blood on a shoe, and a charge slip for his air fare to Montreal that day. We can prove he killed Summers.'

'You know what, Salter,' Orliff said after a few minutes. 'I wouldn't put in all this bullshit about squash and all. I'd put, "From the beginning I had considered the possibility that the motive was robbery, and when I came to the missing lottery ticket I surmised from the phone calls that Bailey might have known about the ticket." Never mind the rest. Keep it simple.'

'Yes, sir.'

'This is very nice, Salter, very nice. What about all the professors you locked up? One of them is suing us for unlawful arrest. Any problem?'

'I don't think so. That's a whole mess which got in the way, although without them I wouldn't have got on to Summers's big win. These people were all diddling each other while Summers was being killed, but it didn't have anything to do with Bailey. I'll tell Dunkley that the charge of obstructing police is still outstanding, or rather, I'll tell his lawyer. He'll understand.'

'Right. I'll tell *you*, Salter, the Old Man is happy. Your pal in Montreal has written us a letter saying how great you are—brilliant, co-operative—all that kind of stuff. The Old Man is so happy he's wondering if we can find a better spot for you, better than you've had for a year.'

In the distance shimmered the oasis, no longer a mirage, but the real thing, with water, dates, and maybe his own camel. Salter said nothing.

'He doesn't hold grudges,' the Superintendent said, 'Longer than necessary, that is. Nor do I. All right, then.' He nodded to dismiss the inspector.

They were parked near the boardwalk down by the Lakeshore. He had phoned her and picked her up after work to say goodbye. They bought some fish and chips at Nova's and sat eating in the car.

'You know,' he said, 'I read Professor Summers's journal. You cropped up a lot. I think he was more interested in you than you realized.'

'You think? But he didn't want to do anything about it. We were just having a little romance without tears. He might have been a bit soft on me, but it was mainly my beautiful mind he liked.'

Probably. He said, 'He wrote once that he would like to have seen you without your pants on.'

'He wrote that, did he?' she laughed.

'Yes. I know what he meant.'

'Well, hello, Charlie!'

'No, no. I think he just meant that he had always seen you in jeans.' Salter thought of the girl on the table in Montreal. 'I've seen you when you weren't wearing them, once.'

'When?'

'At the funeral, remember?'

There was a knock on the car window. A uniformed policeman wanted to talk to him. Salter rolled the window down and showed the officer his identification.

'Sorry, sir.' The policeman saluted. 'We've had a lot of complaints about couples parked here.' He looked pointedly at Molly.

'This is my daughter, Officer. We are just eating some fish and chips.'

'Right, sir. Right.' The man moved off.

'And now,' he said, to the giggling girl, 'I'll take you home.'

Later that night he lay in bed talking to his wife.

She said, 'It isn't the way you think of professors, is it?'

'How do you mean?'

'The way you tell it, he got killed because he won a squash game. Is that normal?'

'No, but I understand how it can happen.'

'And this annual event at the conference? A bit stagey, isn't it?'

'You mean literary.'

'Do I? And these young female students. I think the wives of middle-aged professors must put up with a lot.'

Salter reached over and put his hand on her belly. 'Shut up, now,' he said. She put her hand on his, and after a few moments they rolled together, and made love in friendly, missionary fashion, as he kept his weight on his elbows like a gentleman. He concentrated on her pleasure and joined her when she was ready. Afterwards, as she curled herself around him, she muttered something into his back. 'What?' he asked over his shoulder. She leaned over and kissed him. 'I said that was nice. By the way, someone called Harry Wycke phoned. He wanted us to go for a drink at his house on Saturday night. I told him I thought you were busy. That right? Who is he?'

'He's in Homicide. I think we might go.'

'But, Charlie, we never socialize with the people you know at work.'

'We never used to. Maybe we should give it a try. Wycke seems OK. Now shut up and go to sleep.'

Wisely, she pretended to.

For a biographical note about the author please turn the page.

About the Author

Born in England, Eric Wright came to
Canada as a young man. He lived for a
year in the North, on Hudson's Bay,
before entering the University of
Manitoba where he paid his way by
working on construction sites and as a
fishing guide.

For some years he has lived in Toronto
where he is a teacher. He is married with
two daughters. When not teaching or
writing, he spends his time fishing and
re-reading his favourite novels. He has
written for magazines and TV. *The Night
the Gods Smiled* is his first novel.

ONE MAN'S MEDICINE
Morris Gibson
Foreword by James Herriot

"This is not simply a recital of a doctor's cases, vivid and exciting though they are, it is a warm, funny, touching book. Episodic in character and filled with lovely punch lines it dips into the lives of coal miners, hardy fishermen, and countless ordinary people." So writes James Herriot in his foreword to Morris Gibson's story of his years in medicine.

Dr. Gibson now lives on Vancouver Island. From 1955-78 he practised medicine in Alberta, first as a physician in the foothills of town of Okatoks, later as a professor at the University of Calgary Medical School. But his career in medicine had started in the years just before WW2 in Scotland where he studied at the University of Glasgow, and where he met his wife, herself a medical student.

From student, to graduate, to army doctor, to physician in private practice, the chapters flow happily along giving a kaleidoscopic picture of a country and a people in war and in peace. At the heart of the book are the postwar years the Gibsons spent as young doctors building up a practice in the old and much bomb-damaged Yorkshire seaport of Hull.

A Totem Book

OTHER PEOPLE'S MONEY
The Banks, the Government and Dome
Peter Foster

This is the story of two men and a single ambition: to make Dome Petroleum the world's greatest oil company. The men were Jack Gallagher, Dome's chairman, and Bill Richards, its president. Gallagher was a uniquely charming man with one consuming objective—to make the world's biggest oil strike in the Beaufort Sea.

However, the Beaufort was only part of the Dome dream. The other half was of pure corporate muscle, of multi-billion dollar megaprojects and takeovers. That was the dream of Bill Richards, who master-minded one of the most spectacular bouts of corporate expansion and acquisition ever seen. But then the world economies suddenly shifted and not just Dome but the Canadian banking community that had so indulged the company were brought to the brink of financial disaster.

Peter Foster, the author of *The Blue-Eyed Sheiks* and *The Sorcerer's Apprentices*, is Canada's top writer on finance, on petroleum and on government energy policy. He is uniquely qualified to write this fascinating, controversial and most important book.

A Totem Book

Now available in trade paperback...

VOYAGE OF THE STELLA
R.D. Lawrence

This is the story of the author's six-month solitary exploration of the coasts of British Columbia and the northwestern United States on board his twenty-four-foot cruiser, the *Stella Maris*. Although no stranger to the sea, he found living afloat even more challenging than he had anticipated. He had set out to study the all the creatures of the Pacific, but it was his contact with the largest creatures that inspired the fear and elation that made him so aware of his own mortality, but at the same time so joyfully alive.

Lawrence's relationship with a killer whale he called Klem was one of his most extraordinary experiences with animals in the wild. He had almost equally dramatic encounters with other denizens of the deep, fending off a shark with his bare fists, having an octopus literally eat out of his hands, and playing with an enormous school of porpoises. In this book, the author recaptures the sights, sounds and smells of the awesome Pacific. He brings to this seagoing adventure the same warmth and concern for living things so notable in all his previous books.

A Totem Book

Now available in trade paperback...

THE GHOST WALKER
R.D. Lawrence

In the fall of 1972, the author built a small cabin in the heart of British Columbia's Selkirk Mountains from which to observe the cougar—one of North America's most elusive big game animals. For ten months, the author neither saw nor spoke with another human being, as he tracked the cougar, even accompanying it as it stalked its prey.

By the time Lawrence left the wilderness, he had not only learned a great deal about how the cougar lives in its natural state, but he had won the trust of two members of the species. More than the tale of a special relationship between a man and a wild animal, however, this is also the story of Lawrence's survival alone in a perilous and unforgiving wilderness.

A Totem Book

Now available in trade paperback...

THE ZOO THAT NEVER WAS
R.D. Lawrence

The author and his wife did not plan to become keepers of a wild menagerie when they bought their 350-acre Ontario farm. But, in the absence of an alternative haven for sick and wounded wild animals, they found their home becoming a 'zoo', as they took in and cared for a variety of creatures. Their first wards were a pair of baby raccoons found starving by the side of the road. They were joined by others: Penny, a skunk; Manx, a lynx; a pair of otters; a porcupine; and many more. The most endearing and troublesome member of the zoo was Snuffles, a baby bear cub raised in the Lawrence home. This is a story filled with scientific lore, as well as humour, warmth and adventure.

A Totem Book

Also available in TOTEM CRIME